LOVE STRUCK

ALLY BLOOM

AZALA ROMANCE

1

___

CHARLIE

THURSDAY, JUNE 15TH: 1:30 A.M.

AIDEN'S MOUTH IS MOVING, but I can't make out the words. While he goes on about Wall Street like he's some big shot investor, I've been carefully counting the freckles on his face. It's this game I play when I get bored of our conversation, though I've never successfully completed a count. So far, I note at least 65 freckles across the bridge of his tanned nose and cheeks.

You'd think I'd have every mark on my fiancé's skin memorized by now, but I don't. Each time I play this little game, I have to start over because I forget where I left off.

We've been engaged for two years and dated for two before that. He's handsome, successful, and charming *when he wants to be*—perfect on paper. To our family and friends, we're already married.

I look down at my glass to check the ice cubes. Watching them slowly melt into my drink makes me giddy. The water diluting the purple liquid makes the glass look like a lava lamp I had as a kid.

The loud crowd blends into the sound of the music, embracing my body like a warm blanket. I love this bar; it feels like one you would see in a rom-com. It's a Tiki-themed

I

speakeasy made to look like a dark cave lined with pink and yellow Christmas lights. Plastic flowers dangle from the ceiling like wild vines, reminding me of an adults-only version of The Rainforest Café.

The crowd is still pretty full for a weeknight, but I guess that's normal for a small college town. The bars in Redwell are usually filled with 20-somethings taking advantage of their new-found freedom.

"Hey." Aiden crudely snaps his fingers in front of my face. I hate it when he does that. It reminds me of my days as a wait-ress, when rude men would snap to get me to come to their table. "You ready to go?" He belches.

"Oh, yeah. Good idea. I'm getting kind of tired." The room spins ever so slightly as I try to hop down from the tall barstool. The various colored lights blur together to form a soft orange hue. Aiden grabs me tightly by the hand and leads us toward the front of the bar, aggressively swaying with each step as he pulls me through hordes of drunk students. Several hot, damp bodies press against mine as we try to squeeze through the narrow doorway leading us outside.

The cool desert air feels crisp on my skin and instantly dries the beads of sweat forming on my hairline.

I've become a night owl since moving to Arizona. I'm from a coastal town in California; it's the only time I can actually handle the temperature outside. I also work the graveyard shift at the hospital, so my mental clock keeps me awake even on my nights off.

"I'll order us a car," I say as I pull out my phone.

"No." He shakes his head. "I didn't drink that much."

"Yes, Aiden. Let me just call a car. You've been drinking a lot." I raise my hand. "It'll be quick."

"I'm fine, Charlie," he snaps back. His tightened jaw and flared nostrils say he won't budge.

I'd really prefer to be picked up, but Aiden gets angry whenever I suggest it. He says alcohol hardly affects him, so there's no need to pay someone else to drive us. We've argued about it dozens of times, but tonight, I don't have the energy. Work was unusually hectic this week, and alcohol makes me drowsy.

"Fine." I give up. "Just get me to bed," I whine as I drag my feet over the parking lot gravel. The dusty purple neon sign spelling out 'The Hot Spot' angrily buzzes above us, as if lecturing the group of moths fluttering around it.

"I know," Aiden grunts back. "Hurry up and get in." He rolls his eyes as he swings open the passenger door.

"What a gentleman," I scoff as I fall onto the cold leather seat. I slide the backrest down so I can doze off during the drive home.

My body jolts back as he floors it out of the parking lot, gravel grinding beneath the tires. I can feel us building speed once we hit the smooth pavement. My head feels like it's dragging behind the rest of my body while each turn rocks my stomach like we're on a boat in rough waters.

"Slow down," I groan. "Why are you driving so crazy?" I sit back up and roll my window down to fight the motion sickness.

"I'm not driving crazy. You're just drunk," he says matter-of-factly.

"Don't tell me I'm drunk! I don't need to be sober to know you're driving erratically." I cross my arms tightly. I can't stand when he acts like I'm being dramatic.

"Okay. Do you want to drive?" he hisses as he points at me. "If you're so annoyed by my driving, maybe you should be the one taking us home!"

We don't spend many nights out at the bars, but when we do, it tends to end in petty arguments like this one.

Aiden mumbles something under his breath as he pushes harder on the gas. I feel like we're traveling at light speed now, and I need to trick my brain into not puking. Maybe he's right. Maybe I *am* drunker than I thought.

I close my eyes again and rest my head against the cold plastic of the door, the wind against my face from the open window both soothing and suffocating.

We slow slightly before turning right. Even though my eyes are closed, I know we're almost home; I've driven this route a thousand times before.

A loud bang against the hood of our car rips me from my thoughts. My hand shoots for the overhead handle as the car jumps over what feels like a speedbump, fingers tightly wound, as if this will single handedly protect me.

"Oh my God, stop the car! What was that?" I shout, blood draining from my face. We come to a screeching halt about twenty feet away.

"I-I think you hit something," I stutter.

Aiden puts his arm over the passenger seat as he turns his head back toward the rear window. "No. I don't see anything." His voice trembles as he looks into the dark void behind us. I can see the fear in his eyes too.

"We need to go check." I start to unbuckle my seatbelt, but Aiden's eyes shoot in my direction.

"Are you crazy?" His voice cracks. He snatches the buckle out of my hand and forces it back into the lock.

"What are you doing? We need to go out there and make sure we didn't hurt someone!" I plead.

Aiden scrunches his blond brows and purses his lips as he thinks over the situation. "Okay," he says with a long sigh. "I'll go check and come back." He swings open the door. "But wait here," he instructs, stumbling out of the car, leaving his door wide open before cautiously walking toward the lump in the road.

The rush of cold air and adrenaline wakes me up. The car

dings in his absence, as if calling for its owner to return and somehow slowing time. Ding... Ding... Ding...

Oh my God. This can't be happening. I can't believe he did this. *I can't believe I let him do this!* I look in the rearview mirror at my fiancé's shadow. His dark figure grows smaller in the distance. He appears to bend over for a moment to examine something in the road before straightening and speed-walking back to the car.

Aiden jumps into his seat and stomps his foot on the gas without buckling up again. This can't be a good sign.

"What was it?" I ask. "Was it a person?"

He begins moaning loudly, like an injured animal, like he's trying to speak but can't.

"What was it?" I repeat as hot tears stream down my face. "Did we hit a person, yes or no?"

He looks at me with glossy eyes. "Yes," he utters.

My heart sinks. We left a human being on the road, injured, possibly dead. How could we do this? "Stop the car. We need to go back," I say.

He shakes his head frantically. "No. No. No," he groans. "We can't do that! Do you want to go to jail? We can't. The house is right around the corner. We need to hurry and put the car in the garage before anyone sees us." His knuckles go white as he tightens his grip on the steering wheel.

"Stop the car, or I'll jump out!" I threaten. "We need to help them. We need to call the police!"

That's when he realizes I'm serious. The car swerves toward the sidewalk and comes to a screeching halt at the end of the block. "Fine. If you need to help him, be my guest. I'm going to park the car and run back to you." His voice goes deep. "Don't tell the cops anything 'til I get there."

I ignore his comments and jump out of the car. Luckily, I chose to wear short block heels tonight. I sprint back to the street corner with all the power in my being. My feet and thighs feel like they're on fire by the time I reach the bloodied body in the road. It takes a moment for my mind to comprehend what I'm looking at.

I tumble to my knees beside the person, the jagged blacktop scraping away my skin in the process. A man is lying on his back in a pool of blood.

I'm stumbling over my phone to turn on the flashlight to inspect his injuries. He's unconscious, breaths shallow.

"Sir, can you hear me?" I say loudly. "You're going to be alright!"

Still no response.

I lift my shaky fingers and somehow manage to dial 9-1-1.

"911. What's the address of your emergency?" a woman with a nasally voice answers.

"Yes, hello. My name is Charlette Damascus, and there's been an accident. We need an ambulance on the corner of High Street and Washington Avenue." My voice nearly gives out as I try to get my breathing under control.

"Okay. Can you tell me what happened? Who's injured?"

I check his pulse. "I don't know him, but there's an unconscious male lying in the street with several shallow lacerations to his left arm and leg," I explain. "I think his right leg might be broken too," I add after further examination.

"Okay. Officers are on the way and should be there in a few minutes. In the meantime, please stay on the line."

I ignore her and mute my microphone. If the operator is still speaking, I can't hear her.

I've treated hundreds of patients with injuries like these in the Intensive Care Unit, but I would have never imagined being the cause of them.

I point my phone's flashlight back at the man. He's wearing running shoes with blood-soaked Nike Crew socks, gray cotton shorts ending just above the knee, and a tattered black long-sleeve shirt. He was obviously working out, but why so late? And why in the middle of an unlit street? I take a deep breath to try to stop myself from spiraling.

His face is covered in blood and dirt, so I can't see the full extent of his wounds, but it's safe to assume he has a concussion and other internal injuries.

I take off my jean jacket and gently place it under his head, hovering my right ear slightly above his mouth so I can listen to his breathing. His lungs sound restricted as he struggles to inhale, so I roll him to his side to help keep his airway open until help arrives.

Guilt and anger wash over me. How could this have happened?

I look around for Aiden, terrified of being alone right now. What if he doesn't come back? What would I say? I feel like a child left at the checkout counter as their parent runs off to find a last minute item.

I try to push the thought out of my mind so I can focus on the person in front of me. I need to keep him stable while we wait for the paramedics. I sit on the road beside him, patiently waiting for sirens or lights. I tuck my tangled dark hair behind my ears so I can get a better look at him, and I can tell there's a handsome face buried beneath the blood and grime from the road.

His left eye twitches simultaneously with the left corner of his mouth, like he could be waking up.

"Hello. Can you hear me?" I ask again. "An ambulance is on the way." I gently place my hand on his side to make sure he doesn't roll onto his back. A knot forms in my throat as I look at the battered person before me, and I try my hardest not to burst into tears.

A pair of stomping feet approach me, Aiden is out of breath

and disheveled, half of his white button-up shirt tucked into his pants while the other half flaps in the wind. His eyes are wide, face pale as a ghost. He's terrified but, like me, is trying to pull himself together.

"Why did you drive off like that? Now we're going to look like we're hiding evidence!" I shout. "The police will be here any minute. We need to tell them the truth." I bring my voice back down to a whisper. "I'm sure everything will be okay if we just fess up now."

Aiden hunches over and rests his hands on his knees. "No," he lets out between gasps, leaning against an old wooden fence. Once he gets his breathing under control, he speaks again. "We need to tell the cops we found him like this. We didn't see the car. We can't describe the car because we didn't see it."

"What the hell are you talking about?" I fire back quickly.

"Shh!" He points to the unconscious man beside me as if he was secretly listening in.

"Look," he starts, "what's done is done. I already—" He stops talking at the sound of sirens in the distance.

I don't want to move the jogger off the street out of fear of hurting him more. "Aiden! Go flag them down. I can't move him out of the way!" I scream frantically.

After what feels like an eternity, red and blue lights appear at the end of the street, sirens growing louder as they approach. Aiden runs to do as he's told, flailing his arms while jumping up and down to get their attention.

An ambulance arrives first, followed by a police car. Within minutes, a pair of young men in blue uniforms have the injured man strapped to a gurney and loaded into their truck, leaving my denim jacket and a dark pool of blood in his place.

I grab my dirtied coat and sit on the curb beside Aiden, who's waiting for someone to take our statements. Two officers, a man and a woman, step out of their patrol vehicle. The tall man talks first. "Hello. Which one of you called?" he asks with a straight face, as if this is just an ordinary day in the office for him.

"Um...that would be me, sir. My name is Charlette Damascus. This is my fiancé, Aiden Beckett."

The officer's eyes remain glued to his notepad. "Can you tell us what happened?"

I open my mouth to tell him what happened. "Well, sir—"

Aiden cuts me off. "We were walking home and found that guy lying in the road. We stopped to help him and called you guys right away," he says calmly.

I look at Aiden in disgust. Are we really doing this right now? Should I call him out and tell the truth? Or will the fact that he's lying and hid the car just make it worse? My mind feels scrambled as I try to figure out the best course of action.

"Did you see the car that hit him or hear any noises?" the man in uniform follows up.

"No sir. We didn't see any cars," Aiden answers a little too eagerly. "I heard tires screeching but didn't think anything of it. I figured it was just some dumb college kids street racing." He lets out a nervous laugh. The lies pour out of his mouth so effortlessly, even I would believe him had I not experienced the crash myself.

"And around what time did you hear that sound?" The officer looks up from his pad.

Aiden shoots a glance to me. "Um, what time would you say that was?" He rubs his chin as if to think. "Maybe 10 or 15 minutes before we called you? I don't know exactly what time that was." He shrugs.

The officer's eyes move to Aiden. "What were you guys doing out so late?" he asks, pale eyes narrowing in suspicion.

"I work the graveyard shift at the hospital as an RN," I jump in without thinking, "so I'm normally awake at this time. Aiden and I live just around that corner there and wanted to go for a walk." There's no turning back now; I guess I'm officially an accomplice.

The officer looks to his partner and waves her over, a short, narrow woman with a slicked back blonde bun. "Please leave your contact information with Officer Bauer here. We'll call you if we have any more questions," he says before walking away.

2

———

CHARLIE

THURSDAY, JUNE 15TH:3:02 A.M.

I MUST HAVE BLACKED out on the short walk home, because one moment, we were with the cops, and the next, I'm standing mindlessly in our dark kitchen.

Once I snap back to reality, I sprint to the other side of the room and swing open our garage door. The fluorescent ceiling lights expose a large dent in the hood of Aiden's four-door sedan and a couple of smaller ones in the right front fender. Luckily, the paint is a dark charcoal gray, so the damage isn't too noticeable.

"It's fucked," Aiden says from behind me, peering over my shoulder.

"We're fucked," I utter back.

"What are we going to do?" Aiden's voice cracks; he's like a small child asking for help after breaking Mom's favorite lamp. "You're gonna need to clean it." He looks at me wide eyed.

He can't be serious. "Don't you mean 'we'?" I ask.

"Babe, I don't have time to stay up and help with this. I have work in the morning and need to get to bed. This is your night off," he says defensively. "Just wipe up the blood. We can figure

II

out the dents later," he says, as if it's just a small task. "I can take your car to work tomorrow."

My stomach churns at his request. *Just wipe up the blood.* As if it's just some spilled milk. His words echo in my mind. Does he understand what he's asking? Or better yet, does he even care?

"You're better at this stuff anyway. I would just get in the way." He tries to kiss me on the cheek, but I shrug him off.

"I'm sorry. I really need to get to bed." He groggily yawns as he trudges down the dark hall into our bedroom, obviously unphased by my rejection. Of course, he's going to bed. I roll my eyes.

I look back at the vehicle to get a closer look at the damage and spot some blood in the center of the largest dent. Small red spots also line the fender. My throat tightens as I look at it. *You made your bed. Time to lie in it.* I forcefully swallow my guilt, stand, and walk back into the kitchen in search of cleaning supplies.

I fill our mop bucket with hot water and dish soap then grab an old sponge and some paper towels. I can't do this outside in the open, so I'll need to make sure I'm keeping the mess to a minimum.

I sit on my knees and start scrubbing, the cold cement offering minor relief to my burning, scraped up legs.

Our garage door is an old-fashioned wooden panel we lift manually. Normally, I hate it due to the inconvenience, but I guess it's good in this instance. It's silent to open, and there's no windows, so no one in the neighborhood can see what I'm doing.

I submerge my sponge in the hot bucket of water and slap the sudsy surface onto the car. The blood is already drying to the paint, making it harder to wipe off. Scrubbing in small circles seems to be the most effective way of cleaning it off.

I look down at my aching, blood-stained fingertips and fall

to my butt in exhaustion. What am I going to do about this mess? There's bloody water everywhere—on my hands, cleaning supplies, even my clothes.

I toss the sponge and paper towels into a poorly constructed fire pit in our backyard before dumping the pink water into our bathtub. We'll need to remember to light a bonfire tonight. I make a mental note.

I take a deep breath before moving on to my next task: the dents. There's one large crater in the hood and two smaller ones in the fender. It looks simple enough, but I don't want to make it worse. I consider watching a tutorial online, but I don't want to risk it. I can just imagine my Google search history plastered on a poster board and used against me as evidence.

The thought makes the hairs on the back of my neck stand.

I remember seeing a video online where a guy fixed a dent in his car using tape. That seems like it would work better than a hammer; less conspicuous too. But won't that chip the paint? If I screw this up, we could go to jail.

In need of a break, I stand and twist, releasing an echo of cracks from my spine. I walk back into the house to check on Aiden and find him sleeping peacefully on the bed. How can he sleep so easily as I clean up his mess?

Maybe I should just confess to the cops and tell them what really happened. I'll bet they'll go easier on me for telling the truth. I mean, I did help our victim, and that has to count for something, right?

Snap out of it. It's too late to come clean. I've already done too much. My head is spinning.

I brew myself a single cup of coffee and fall onto the couch for some much needed rest. The stress and chaos of tonight is finally catching up with me, my tired bones aching as I relax my muscles to melt into the cushions. It's already 4 in the morning, but I don't have work today, so it doesn't matter.

I typically work three to four twelve-hour shifts a week, depending on how short-staffed we are. While the long work days suck, the three-day weekends almost always make up for it.

I look at my phone and scroll mindlessly through social media, praying it temporarily soothes my frayed nerves.

Aiden's loud snores carry through the hall. How can he sleep at a time like this? My mind is consumed with so many thoughts, I can hardly sit still. My left leg bounces without my permission like an addict waiting for the next fix. I fold my legs and scoot back on the sofa with my hot cup of liquid fuel. Coffee is the last thing my anxiety needs, but I could really use the energy boost. I take a deep gulp of the vanilla goodness and melt into my seat.

That's it. Break time is over.

I search unsuccessfully through our kitchen junk drawer for the duct tape, though if I needed buttons, Ibuprofen, batteries, and lint, I would be in luck.

Great. This drawer has everything but the one thing I actually need.

Maybe something with suction will work? I head to the bathroom to examine our toilet plunger. It looks around the same size as the dent in the hood. I take it to the garage to compare it to the crater on his car. Et *voila! It's the perfect size.*

I push the plunger into the dent and unintentionally make the crater double in size. The loud pop of the hood makes my heart skip a beat. Oh no; did I just make this worse? I close my eyes and take a deep breath. "Just trust the process," I whisper to myself skeptically.

I plant my left foot on one side of the hood to give myself leverage as I yank the plunger back up. My back nearly seizes as

I try to pull the dent out, but after a few good tugs, it finally pops back into place like a clap of thunder. Hopefully, the bang didn't wake anyone in the neighborhood.

I honestly can't believe that worked. It's like a weight has been lifted off my chest. The other dings may be too small for the plunger, but I'm sure I can just hammer those ones out later. Maybe I can wrap a rag around the hammer to help silence the blows. Regardless, I'll wait a few hours before trying that out. I don't want anyone to complain about the banging.

I collapse in both exhaustion and relief, sprawling across the cold floor. The silence in the garage echoes in my ears. It's that funny time of day when most people are still sleeping but the birds are starting to wake up and chirp. My body has never felt so sore, each limb too heavy to lift. I think I've done as much work to the car as I can in one sitting.

I drag myself to our bedroom and find Aiden, arms and legs spread across the bed, as if trying to protect his territory. It takes all my strength to move his large leg back to his side of the bed. I fall into the small sliver of space next to him, sheets warm and comforting from his body heat, close my eyes, and my mind finally goes blank.

I wake up to an empty bed. I guess Aiden already left for work, in my car, I assume. I stretch out like a starfish, fingers and toes widespread. The morning feels rather peaceful. For a moment, I forget about the chaos of just a few hours ago. It all feels like a distant bad dream. I look around the room and wait for the rest of my body to wake up.

Gold streams of sunshine pour through the blinds, illuminating the dust particles in the air. The birds are going about their usual morning conversations. The beauty quickly fades, however, when I return to the garage.

The dented bumper stares at me as if to mock me. I examine the dents and imagine the person who created them. Which part of his body made this one? Whoever he is, he didn't go down without a fight.

The thought makes me nauseous. I need to know if he's okay. It's safe to assume he was admitted to the hospital where I work, since the only other one is two towns away. Maybe I can check on him during my shift tomorrow. Except...I have no idea who he is. I'll ask someone from work. Who was on shift last night?

I grab my phone off the charger so I can text one of my co-workers. It looks like the word is already out.

> Hey. What happened last night?

> Hey! I heard about what happened. He's lucky you were there! He's stable right now. Hopefully, they catch the lunatic who did it.

> You can't seem to escape work, can you?

One of the EMTs must have recognized me last night. Word travels fast around here. All the first responders and medical personnel seem to know each other. It kind of feels like high school with all the cliques.

I respond to Erica, who is basically my work mom, and ignore the rest of the messages.

> Hey. Yeah, last night was crazy. How does everyone know about it?

Three dots appear on my screen and then disappear.

Oh, right, Shawn, Sheila's paramedic boyfriend I've only met a couple of times. I'm surprised he even recognized me, considering how dark it was.

The thought of all my coworkers talking about me is frightening. What if they get suspicious? Did Shawn suspect anything? The question makes my stomach churn, and I slap my hand over my mouth to keep myself from throwing up.

In desperate need of a cool down, I make myself a cup of green tea and run myself a hot bath to relax. What's the point of doing all this if I end up dying from a heart attack anyway?

I submerge my body in the warm, sudsy water, lay my head back, and close my eyes as the aroma of fresh lavender and eucalyptus fills the air.

I'm trying to convince myself everything will work out. *You didn't kill anyone. You weren't driving, so you're not liable. You'll be okay. Aiden's at fault here.* Deep down, though, I know I'm wrong. "You will be okay," I quietly say out loud to myself.

This will be my new mantra.

A loud buzz interrupts my bath thoughts, so I peek at my phone to see Erica calling.

"Hello?" I answer.

"You didn't hear it from me, but the patient's name is Henry Ryner, room 1032," Erica says.

"Thanks, Erica," I say.

"No problem, sugar. Gotta run." She hangs up.

My heart sinks as I finally put a name to the battered face I saw on that dark street. Henry. His name is Henry Ryner.

I immediately open Instagram and type in the name. There are a few Henry Ryners but only one in Arizona. His profile picture is with his dog. The image is too small to tell, but I think it's a goldendoodle. I click on his username to see more photos, but instead, I reach a gray wall that says 'Private Account.' There's no way I can request to follow him. *Shit.*

I check Facebook to see if he has any pictures. Does anyone even post there anymore? After scrolling through a few names, I finally find the right one. The last photo he uploaded is from five years ago.

He looks much skinnier than the man I saw last night, with neatly combed brown hair and dark brown eyes. He's clean-shaven, with a slight dimple on his chin. Seeing his face sends shivers through my body.

These images remind me he's a real person with a real life, not just some faceless figure on the road. My chest tightens as I stare remorsefully at my screen, lungs straining with each inhale. How will I ever cope? I've done something terrible, and this man's life could be ruined because of it. I'm exhausted, my soul feels drained and my heart is numb.

I wonder how Aiden is handling all of this.

3

AIDEN

THURSDAY, JUNE 15TH: 8:30 A.M.

THIS IS SHIT. I can't focus on work right now; my brain is all over the place. I've been staring mindlessly at this blank Excel sheet all morning, only occasionally moving my mouse to look busy. I may have drank too much last night, but that guy came out of nowhere! What was I supposed to do? I couldn't avoid him.

Fuck.

I hope Charlie was able to fix up the car. Maybe I'll swing by the house on my lunch break and check, unless that's too suspicious. A text or call may be less obvious.

"Knock, knock." Lexi, our office assistant, pokes her silky blonde head over my cubicle wall. "How's it going?" she asks with a bright smile.

Lexi is always dressed to the nines, though with minimal makeup. She embraces her natural beauty, and *beautiful* she is. Today, she's wearing a flowy white shirt with blue jeans that hug her ass just right. It's obvious she does Pilates.

"Oh, it goes," I joke, trying to mask the stress in my voice. "What's up?"

She walks around my cubicle and leans her round hip

against the side of my desk. She's wearing open toed heels, showcasing her white nail polish that makes her skin look perfectly tanned.

"Alex says he needs your report by Friday now. He wants to look it over before his meeting Monday. Just thought I would give you a heads up," she chirps.

"Oh, thanks." I nod.

"Are you okay?" She takes a step closer, gently placing her hand on my shoulder. "You seem a bit out of it today."

"Oh. Yeah, I'm okay. I just had a rough night." I fake a laugh, trying hard not to stare at her breasts at eye level.

"Okay. Well, let me know if you need anything," she says before turning back to her desk, leaving a sweet trail of coconut body spray in her wake.

I let out a long sigh, grateful for the brief encounter. I don't really feel like talking to anyone today, especially her. I don't have the energy to keep up with her bubbly personality.

I check my phone to see if I have any new notifications. *Nothing.* Maybe it's a good thing Charlie's not texting me. I think the police can use that in their investigation.

I lean back in my chair and close my eyes for a moment.

Get yourself together, Aiden. The cops have nothing on you. No one saw anything. Well, except for the jogger I ran over. I'm pretty sure he saw my car. But...it was dark outside. He could have easily gotten confused. Plus, he was knocked out, so there's no way he heard us talking, right?

Oh God, what about cameras? Could there have been any street cams? I don't recall seeing any, but maybe I should go for a walk today and scout it out. I'll retrace my steps, starting at the bar. But first, I need to get through this fucking day.

I get home to the sound of 'Friends' on TV and the smell of freshly baked cookies. This is Charlie's go-to comfort combo. She normally saves this for her periods or when she's really anxious, but I guess now is as good of a time as any.

"Hey. How's it going?" I drop my backpack on the kitchen floor and toss my keys on the countertop.

"Hi," she says without looking away from the TV.

"So..." I plop onto the couch cushion next to her. "How's the car looking?"

If her eyes were daggers, I'd be dead. What did I do wrong now? She said she was going to clean it. It's not like I'm forcing her to do it.

"What?" I ask.

She lets out a nasal sigh. "Nothing. It's just the way you asked. Why don't you go to the garage and take a look for yourself?" She shoves another chocolate chip cookie into her mouth and turns up the volume of the TV.

Why does she need to act like this? I just got home; I don't need to hear her bitching already.

I go to the garage to check out the car. Wow, she actually did a pretty good job cleaning it up. I wonder how she did it. The large crater in the hood of the car is now a dent the size of a nickel, and the fender is straightened out for the most part. Maybe she should start changing my oil and rotating my tires too.

I take my time examining it, because I'm not ready to go back inside the house. I don't feel like holding a conversation with anyone, especially if Charlie is going to be in one of her moods all night.

Like everyone, I make mistakes, but she makes sure to point them out. *Stop being so negative, Aiden. Pick up after yourself, Aiden.'* I can't handle any more criticism right now.

I grab a beer from the garage fridge and sit on the step just outside the kitchen door, embracing the much needed silence.

4

CHARLIE

THURSDAY, JUNE 15TH: 5:25 P.M.

No amount of relaxing rids me of the tight knots in my stomach. All those cookies I ate actually made me feel worse. I'm now both stressed and bloated.

I try not to think about the situation, or the fact that Aiden is likely sulking like a child in the garage. Maybe a walk will help clear my head.

The weather should be cooling down now since it's almost sunset. I toss on a white cotton tank top, gray shorts, and pink baseball cap, then head out. Warm air slaps me in the face as I open my front door, instantly drawing beads of sweat under the brim of my hat, the kind that will leave wrinkles on my forehead.

Despite the wretched weather, it's actually quite beautiful outside. The sky looks like a vibrant painting in various shades of pink and orange. The purple mountain range far beyond this little community of houses doesn't even look real, more like a backdrop you would see in an old Hollywood Western film. You'd never guess such a violent crime took place in a scene like this.

The thought of going to work tomorrow makes my palms sweat. What's it going to be like seeing everyone? I assume they'll bombard me with questions I'm not ready to answer.

And what about Henry? Part of me wants to check on him and see if he's okay. The other part of me, *the more rational side,* says to avoid him at all costs. I'm sort of the one who put him there, after all.

"Agh!" A frustrated yelp escapes my chest. I'm having too many thoughts. I feel like someone's squishing my brain through their fingers like raw meatloaf.

I snap out of it to find myself mindlessly approaching the scene where Henry nearly died less than twenty-four hours ago, as if my body wandered here on its own.

A white van sporting the yellow letters KRDC appears from behind the old fence as I round the corner. I freeze, pretending to catch my breath as I try to listen in on the reporter inter-viewing an older gentleman.

"And did you hear anything suspicious last night?" a woman with fluffy black curls points her microphone toward the tired man in a scratchy looking blue bathrobe.

"No, nothin." He scratches his balding gray head. "I was just sleepin' when I got woken up by the police lights shining through my bedroom window there. I just can't believe it."

"Thank you for your time, sir." The reporter pulls away and continues speaking toward the camera. "Reporting live from Redwell for KRDC News, I'm Patricia Hernandez."

"We're clear," the cameraman announces. The woman's charming TV smile instantly melts away as she pulls a mirror from her pocket to inspect her makeup.

KRDC is really here. Everyone in town watches them. The hospital runs their newscasts non-stop in the waiting areas. My knees almost give way at the thought of them being so close to my house.

"Excuse me, miss?"

A woman's voice pulls me out of my head. I was unintention-ally making eye contact with that reporter, and now she's waltzing directly toward me. Her short, stubby cameraman follows behind her like a well-trained dog.

"I'm with KRDC News. I'm reporting on the hit-and-run that happened early this morning. Do you live around here?" she asks eagerly.

"Oh, uh." I take a step back. "Yeah, I do. But I don't know anything."

"That's okay. Would you mind if I ask you some questions? I'm trying to—"

"I'm sorry, I'm actually in a rush." I turn around and start walking before she has the chance to say anything else. The small woman looks unphased by my rejection and quickly turns away, leading her cameraman to a pair of nosy onlookers a few yards away.

She's bound to find someone who heard or saw something. What if there was a witness?

I don't know how long I can keep this terrible secret to myself. It's consuming me. How can I go to work tomorrow? I'm supposed to be someone who helps people, not a willing accom-plice in a violent hit-and-run. There's no way I can look my colleagues in the eyes again.

I take a deep breath and count to ten, trying my best to compose myself. The dry heat of the desert air stings my lungs as I inhale, telling me it's time to go back home. I can only imagine what my hair looks like under this damp baseball cap.

"Where were you?" Aiden jumps up from the couch dramatically, as if I've been gone for days.

"I went for a walk. Is something wrong?" I ask.

"Yeah, well, we have a lot going on right now. The least you can do is tell me if you're leaving the house." He rubs his hands through his dirty blonde hair as he plops back down in his seat. I can tell he's just as stressed as I am.

"Okay, sorry. You were out in the garage, so I didn't think to tell you." I toss my sweat-drenched hat on the kitchen counter and pour myself a glass of water. The ceiling fan immediately cools my damp head.

"So, uh..." I say between gulps. "I'm not trying to freak you out more than you already are, but, uh, I ran into a news van outside." I try to brace myself for his reaction, but to my surprise, he stays silent.

Aiden is sitting hunched over on the couch, lifeless, apparently unphased. What's going through his mind?

"Hey. Are you okay?" I ask.

"Huh? Oh, yeah. I'm fine. Just thinking," he replies without making eye contact.

"Did you hear what I said?" I ask.

"Yeah, the news..."

"Oh, okay. You don't have any feeling about journalists sniffing around?"

"Jesus Christ, Charlie!" he snaps. "Can't I have a few minutes without you questioning me?" He jumps to his feet and walks to our bedroom, slamming the door behind him.

I guess we all have our own ways of dealing with issues, and Aiden's way has never included talking through it. Our fights usually consist of senseless yelling followed by icing each other out until someone, usually me, caves and apologizes. We never actually reach a real resolution; we just sweep it under the rug and forget.

I pour myself a glass of wine and take his place on the couch, the cushion still warm from his body. The thought of a camera crew makes me uneasy, so I turn on my TV show and pull out my phone to push the thought out of my head.

Before I realize it, I find myself mindlessly scrolling through Henry's outdated Facebook photos again, examining his face for the tenth time. I can't seem to get him out of my mind. Does he have anyone at the hospital with him?

I hate that his Instagram profile is private.

Wait. I open the app and quickly switch to my abandoned food profile I created when I wanted to be a blogger. I gave up after only two sad pasta photos; it's hard to be a content creator when you basically live in the hospital.

I unfollow my main account and remove my personal username from the bio so there's no visible connection to me and then request to follow his page. My heart sinks once the blue button turns gray. Is this too obvious? What if the police see I tried to follow him? Would he report this to investigators?

No, I'm just overthinking, like usual.

I toss my phone on the opposite end of the couch and turn up the TV. Hopefully, I can clear my mind enough to fall asleep tonight, especially since I work tomorrow. It's only 9 o'clock, and I'm already feeling tired. My circadian rhythm is so out of whack.

"Hey," a deep voice grunts from the end of the hall. "I'm trying to sleep. Do you mind?" Aiden says before slamming the bedroom door shut again.

I roll my eyes and press arrow on the remote once. Aiden hates sitcoms because of the laugh tracks. He says he shouldn't be told when something is funny, which I guess makes sense, though he also watches golf, so he can't judge me for my TV habits.

I stare at the screen in a daze when a dim glow catches my

eye from the other end of the couch. An unfamiliar feeling settles in the pit of my stomach.

I stretch my body across the couch and set my face next to my phone.

"*Hen.R.y Accepted your Request.*"

I nearly throw up when I read the words. Should I be this excited to see his profile? Am I crossing into psychotic territory?

I push the thought out of my mind and tap the notification, taking me to his Instagram profile. He last posted a picture of a goldendoodle standing in a stream two months ago, with the caption 'Dog sitting.' It looks like he took it while on a canyon hike.

The next one is a group photo at what appears to be a wedding. He's wearing a navy blue blazer and slacks that fit him just right. His hair kind of reminds me of Hugh Grant in *Four Weddings and a Funeral*, and his smile is charming too, much different than the man I saw before.

Images of his battered face flash through my mind. He looks so happy here, and we nearly took that all away.

I spot a leg tattoo in another hiking photo. His shorts are high enough to expose a large, round symbol on his right thigh. It looks sexy as hell and highlights his muscular build, but I can't quite make out what it is. I try to imagine his body under those clothes and wonder if he has any other tattoos.

Wait—what am I doing? I snap out of my head. My stomach tenses up. Not only did I take part in a crime, but now I'm ogling over a man outside my relationship. What the hell is wrong with me?

I turn off my phone and throw it back on the other end of the couch. I can't allow this guy to distract me. There's too much at stake here, and falling for his good looks won't help the situation.

I bring my knees to my chest and lay in a fetal position,

closing my eyes as I pray that this isn't actually my reality. Hopefully, I'll wake up in the morning and realize this has all been a very long nightmare.

I can feel myself quickly slipping into the dark void, chaotic thoughts slowly fading into the background.

Finally, silence.

5

CHARLIE

FRIDAY, JUNE 16TH: 6:45 P.M.

My blaring phone alarm startles me awake. I try to hit snooze, but, based on the time, I must have done that several times already. As I groan, my heavy body inches toward the edge of the bed, where I sit for a moment and contemplate my life choices. Work feels like a mountain I'm just not ready to climb.

I stretch as I try to get the blood moving through my body. Then, I jump up and head to my bathroom to get ready.

Long hours mean makeup is usually a no-go, but today, maybe a little will help. Not wanting to overdo it, I fluff my already full eyebrows then add a light coat of waterproof mascara, a hint of blush, and pink-tinted chapstick. My thick brown hair gets pulled into a low ponytail. I put on my best scrubs and head out my bedroom door.

Aiden, who I didn't realize was home, is cooking something in the kitchen. I shout "bye" and rush out of the house without waiting for a response. I'm not late or anything, but I don't feel like faking pleasantries. I'm definitely not happy with him right now and don't want to pretend.

He's the one who screwed up, and he has yet to actually do anything helpful. All he's done is bitch and whine while I do his

30

dirty work. Not once has he thanked me or even apologized for his actions. Sometimes, I feel like I live with a toddler.

I can't say that I'm surprised, though. At some point in our relationship, he simply stopped apologizing—or trying, for that matter. I guess in many ways, I have too. Maybe we've just outgrown each other. The thought leaves a pit in my belly.

We started dating the summer after our freshman year of college. It was fun and fresh back then, like any new relationship. He was actually interested in me. But as time went on, his behavior changed. He stopped doing the little things or asking me random questions in the middle of the night. It's as if he slowly became more irritated with his life, with me.

Aiden proposed during my final semester of nursing school. I love him, but I don't remember feeling happy when he asked me to marry him. A big part of me feels like he only did it because it's what our families wanted. If I'm being honest, maybe that's why I said yes.

I let out a long sigh, trying to redirect my attention to the road. I don't need another incident.

Focus, Charlie.

I chant words of affirmation to myself as I pull into the hospital parking lot. "You are strong. You are successful. You are smart." Being stressed at work isn't going to help anyone. I close my eyes and inhale deeply through my nose, out through my mouth.

"Okay," I whisper to myself and grab my bag. I dash through the crowded lobby, trying my best to evade gazes in the waiting room and head straight to the locker room. I don't usually enter through this way, but it was the closest door to my car, and I'm now running late. *Fuck.* I realize I forgot to pack a lunch as I tuck my bag into my locker. I guess I'll have to settle for cafeteria food tonight.

I slam my locker shut and make my way to check my station on our assignment sheet hanging on a corkboard alongside various colorful hospital announcements.

Charlette, section B

B? Isn't Room 1032 in that area? Sweat starts to form under my arms.

That's *his* room...

"Get it together," I swallow. Maybe I can ask our charge nurse, Amanda, to assign him to someone else? But I would need a good reason for that. I'll save his room for last; maybe I can come up with some excuse to hand him off by then.

My feet go numb as I walk toward the nurses' station.

"Good evening, sunshine," Erica says in her sweet southern accent as she walks out of a patient's room. "Aren't you looking nice today?" She smiles suspiciously.

Erica is a middle-aged woman from North Carolina who moved here to be closer to her kids. I'm usually charmed by her sweet demeanor, but today, her compliment falls on deaf ears.

"Oh, yeah." I fake a smile, hoping she doesn't catch the hint of panic in my voice.

"Did you and your fiancé do something fun before work?" She tosses her clipboard on the desk. She crosses her arms and leans her hip against the ledge, waiting for an answer.

"Um, no. I just figured I can't always look like a dumpster fire. HR might write me up," I say a little too sarcastically as I walk to my first patient's room. She smacks her lips as I walk away, but I'll take a sick person over small talk any day.

"Good evening. How are you feeling today?" I ask as I flip through the patient's chart.

Charles, Bradley R.
Age: 75
Reason for visit: hip arthroplasty

"Well, I'm doing a lot better now that you're here," the dark skinned man with a salt and pepper beard says with a charming smile. I can tell he was a ladies' man back in the day.

"That's good to hear, Mr. Bradley. My name is Charlie, and I'll be taking over as your nurse tonight." I smile. "I'm just going to check your vitals real quick. Can I get you some water when I'm done?"

"Ugh, no, that's okay. I'm fine," he grunts uncomfortably.

"Okay. The doctor will be with you soon to check on your incision." I smile and leave. My feet are heavy as I reluctantly walk to the next room, anxious to finally reach Henry.

Work has always been a comforting place. When things aren't going right in my personal life, I can always bury myself in tasks here; there's never a shortage of things to do. But today, work seems to be making my problems abundantly worse.

1032.

I'm as still as a statue as I reread the numbers on the wall to make sure I have the right room. On the other side of this door is the man we nearly killed, and here I am, about to casually walk in as if he were just some ordinary patient.

You got this. You're a professional, I remind myself. If I stand in the hallway any longer, people will think something is wrong. I let out a deep breath and then plaster a fake smile on my face before walking in.

"Knock, knock," I sheepishly announce as I creep into his room. My hands shake as I pull back his bedroom curtain.

"Good evening," I say softly, trying to avoid meeting his eyes. "My name is Charlette, and I'm going to be your nurse tonight."

I feel his heavy gaze follow me as I walk to his bedside and check his chart on the computer. The silence in the room is heavy, the only sounds the monitor and his deep breathing.

"Hey." His deep voice sounds raspy and strained.

"Are you feeling any pain right now?" I ask, keeping my eyes fixed on the screen but watching his movements in my peripheral.

Guilt and shame wash over me when I see the bulky cast on his right leg. He's going to need surgery on his knee, but his doctor wanted to wait for his concussion symptoms to subside before putting him under.

"Not right now, no." He clears his throat.

"Okay, I'll come back in a bit to check on you. You'll be due for another dose of Neoprofen at 9:30." I speed-walk out before he has time to say anything else.

I was so worried about seeing him, I completely forgot what I was doing in there. Did I remember to ask if he needed anything? Did I check his blood pressure? I don't even know. It's like my mind and body were on auto pilot.

This isn't good. I can't even do my job right when I'm around him.

I quietly close his room door behind me and drop my face into my hands. I can't believe this is happening. He's here, my *patient*! Is this my punishment? The sound of shuffling feet and talking nurses slowly fade into the background, leaving only the sound of my intensifying heartbeat.

"How ya doin', hun?" a comforting voice sneaks up from behind, releasing me from my trance. "You okay?" My best friend, Sheila, puts her hand on my shoulder.

"Oh, hey. Yeah. I'm fine, thanks."

She raises her brow in disbelief. "Let's chat later, yeah?" she says as she walks to the supply closet down the hall.

"Yeah. Tonight!" I shout.

6

CHARLIE

FRIDAY, JUNE 16TH: 7:45 P.M.

MY WATCH TAUNTS ME, reminding me it's almost time to check on Henry again, but I don't think I can do it. I need to come up with some excuse to get him reassigned to someone else without being too obvious.

I hesitantly walk to the nurses' station in search of Amanda to see if she can help me out, but I think I already know the answer.

"Amanda?" I cautiously approach the tall bulldozer of a woman.

"Yeah?" she replies without looking up from her computer screen.

"I'm not feeling well. Can you reassign one of my patients? Room 1032, last name Ryner," I say.

Her aggressive clicks against the keyboard stop as she peers up through her glasses. "Why him?" She lifts a thin blonde brow.

"Oh, uh, well...because my other patients don't require as much care," I say.

Her tired gray eyes fall back to her computer screen, and the loud typing resumes. "Sorry, Charlie. We're understaffed. Plus,

36

you have the most knowledge of Mr. Ryner's file, since you treated him on scene," she says unapologetically.

"Okay." I let out a small, disappointed sigh.

She looks back up at me and rolls her eyes. "Go on and take a break," she huffs. "I'll send someone else to check on him this *one time*, but after that, he's yours."

"Thanks, Amanda." My muscles relax as I turn toward the break room.

"Hey, you going on lunch?" Sheila speedwalks to catch up to me.

"Yeah, but I forgot my lunch, so I'll need to get something from downstairs," I say.

"No problem. I'll grab my food and meet you down there." She smiles and walks away.

Sheila is a 6-foot-tall blonde with a cheerful demeanor that can leave even the grouchiest of people in a good mood. That's part of what makes her such an amazing nurse—any patient in her care immediately feels safe.

———

Food options down here are limited at this time of night. Should I go with the dry turkey sandwich with soggy, discolored cheese, or a pre-packaged salad with wilted leaves? I grab the slightly less intimidating chipotle salad bowl and head to a table with Sheila.

My butt barely touches my seat when she cuts straight to the chase.

"So what happened the other night?" she asks as she unzips her leopard print lunch bag. "Shawn told me most of it, but, like, what happened before he got there?"

I was hoping this wasn't going to come up, but I guess it's unavoidable in a small town.

"Oh, right. *That*." I let out a long sigh. "Well, you know I don't sleep well, particularly at night, so I asked Aiden if he would go for a walk with me. Literally just a couple of blocks from our house, we found a guy laying in the middle of the street. Obviously, I checked on him and called the police," I say as I struggle to peel the plastic seal off my salad bowl. I'm afraid she'll know I'm lying if I look into her eyes.

"Wow, that must've been so crazy! So did you hear or see anything?" she asks, wide-eyed. Her hazel eyes shimmer with excitement, as if she's watching some TV drama.

"Um, no," I say nervously. Hopefully, she buys it. "He was by himself when we got there. No one else was around."

"I can't believe some bastard hit him and just drove off! Who the hell does that?" She pouts as she shoves a carrot stick into her mouth.

"Yeah, uh, same," I answer, trying to keep this conversation short.

"So, how's he doing? I saw he was assigned to you." She tries to hide her smile.

"Um, he's okay. I kept it brief. I thought it would be weird if I introduced myself," I grunt as I force a fork full of droopy lettuce into my mouth.

"Well, I think you should. After all, you are the one who saved him. I know if that was me, I would want to meet the beautiful woman who rescued me," she snickers.

"Yeah, maybe." I lean in. "But I'm not sure how I would even bring that up. I don't want to force him to remember something traumatic like that, ya know?"

Sheila leans back as she ponders the situation. "Well, make it casual. You can say 'I'm glad you're feeling better. I was worried when I found you on the road', or something like that." She flicks her wrist.

"Maybe." I entertain her suggestion knowing full well I won't do it. I'm just going to keep my head down and do my job until he's discharged. Then, we'll never have to see each other again.

"You know the girls upstairs are seething with jealousy. They all wanted dibs on the sexy single teacher." She laughs.

"How would you know that?" I scoff.

"Word gets around. If he did have a girlfriend, she would be at his bedside right now. But according to the girls on day shift, only an older woman has visited him."

"Wow, Sheila. You've really been doing your homework." I laugh. I honestly don't know if I should be thrilled or scared by this information.

"He is definitely gorgeous, but I'm engaged, so no gawking for me," I say unenthusiastically.

My friends aren't the biggest fan of Aiden. Maybe it's because they're the ones I vent to about his shitty attitude. It gave them the impression I'm unhappy with him, which I guess isn't too far off.

"Okay. Either way, please tell me how it goes. I'll be expecting a call from you after your shift!" She waves her finger to let me know she's serious.

"Okay, okay." I smile and roll my eyes.

I wonder how many times I'll be asked about this. Gossip travels like wildfire. It's not like Henry is the first crash victim they've seen, but I guess the paramedics made our story sound more interesting than it was. Well, the version we told them, anyway.

My phone alarm goes off, signaling our break is over. A relieved feeling washes over me; I won't have to answer any more questions about Henry. I'm ready to bury myself back in work and forget about this whole situation. I only wish I had eaten something more filling.

7

CHARLIE

SATURDAY, JUNE 17TH: 2:30 A.M.

IT'S OKAY. I close my eyes and take a deep, calming breath. I have no other choice; I need to go in. My sweaty hand slides over the door handle as I try to push it open.

I step quietly into Henry's dimly lit room, careful not to wake him.

It's strange, seeing him like this. His unconscious body brings flashbacks of his limp figure in a puddle of his own blood. I freeze, watching his chest slowly rise and fall under the thin hospital sheet.

Calm down. You can do this. He's asleep. I inch closer to his bedside to check his monitor. He shuffles for a moment, sending ice through my veins, and I freeze, holding my breath until he finishes readjusting his injured leg.

Phew. I turn toward the computer beside his bed.

"Oh, it's you," he says groggily.

I look over to find his sleepy brown eyes watching me. His dark hair is disheveled but still cute, and light scruff covers his cheeks and bruised jaw.

"I'm sorry. I didn't mean to wake you," I whisper.

"No, it's okay." He yawns. "I was hoping to see you again," he says, voice clearing as he perks up.

He wanted to see *me*? "Why?" I take a step back so he doesn't see the worry in my eyes.

"Well, the nurse earlier told me you're the one who saved my life." He presses a button on the side of his bed to lift him up to sit. "Why didn't you say something earlier?" He runs his fingers through his hair to sweep the loose strands out of his face.

"Oh, I-I'm sorry. I guess I didn't want to remind you of that night and bring unnecessary stress," I say.

He cracks a nervous smile, and the dim light beside his bed highlights a small dimple in his chin and right cheek. "No stress at all."

"Uh...how's your pain level?" I ask, trying to move on.

"Well, this is starting to feel uncomfortable," he says, raising his forearm to show me his IV site.

I take a step closer to inspect and see the catheter is dislodged from his forearm, leaving a small pool of blood beneath the transparent tape.

"Ouch. Looks like we're going to need to relocate that," I say.

"Yeah, I figured as much," he groans.

My body feels weak as I prepare my tray of supplies. *I'm about to touch him.* I don't know why that thought scares me so much. It's not like I haven't done this before. I guess I'm just scared to get too close to him, as if my face will trigger his suppressed memories from that night that I don't want resurfacing.

"Okay." I set the tray on the table beside his bed. "This should only take a second."

His skin breaks into goosebumps beneath my fingertips as I gently peel back the tape, sending my stomach into a cartwheel.

"Yikes. That really sticks to the arm hairs, huh?" He releases a soft yet deep belly laugh.

"Yeah, sorry about that," I say as I bandage his right arm. "Are you left handed?"

He cocks his head, as if intrigued by this random question. "Yeah, I am. Why do you ask?"

"Just making sure. We try to avoid putting it on your dominant side if we can help it. I'm going to place it down here, on your right hand instead," I explain.

I grab his heavy hand to feel around for the best vein and can't help but notice it's twice the size of mine. His large fingers drape over my dainty wrist as I search for a spot to place the new IV.

"Okay, this will only take a second. You're going to feel a pinch in 3...2...1."

"You said your name is Charlie, right?" He looks at me curiously, completely ignoring the prick of the needle.

Hearing my name leave his mouth makes me dizzy. "Um, yes."

"Well, thank you, Charlie. I'm feeling better already." He grins.

I take a step back, fearing I'll get trapped in his gaze if I stand too close. "Sure, no problem. Now, get some rest and call me if you need anything." I shuffle backward, slightly stumbling over a power cord on my way out.

"Woah, careful there." He smirks.

My face is burning hot, and I'm feeling flushed. I quickly turn away and bolt to the room next door.

8

———

CHARLIE

SATURDAY, JUNE 17TH: 6:45 A.M.

I EXAMINE my face in a locker room mirror. The little bit of makeup I had on earlier has since sweat off, leaving a slight gray hue underneath my already tired brown eyes. My hair isn't looking too good either. The baby hairs stick to my forehead like I just ran a mile.

I brush my tangled hair and pull it into a claw clip, leaving just two strands of hair hanging by my face. The sweat makes my brown hair look dark and sleek when I pull it back.

I'm going for the natural beauty look, so I re-fluff my eyebrows and put on a fresh layer of mascara, followed by some clear, lip-plumping gloss.

I'm about to make my final rounds of the day, and I figured I should clean up before saying goodbye to my patients....well, *one* patient.

———

As I get closer to Henry's room, I hear voices coming from inside. Does he have guests? No, visiting hours don't start until

43

eight, so it can't be that. I slow my steps and try to listen in without being too conspicuous.

My growing anxiety dissolves at the sound of laughter. "I miss you all too!" Henry's voice is lighter and more enthusiastic than before.

"Bye, Mr. Ryner! Feel better!" the small voices chant, followed by complete silence. It must have been a video call. Mr. Ryner, huh? Is he a teacher?

I'm not sure why, but the fact that he teaches kids intensifies my guilt. We almost took away a person who shapes young minds. How would they have processed learning their teacher was murdered?

My feet stay glued to the floor as I consider my next steps. Sheila's voice pops into my head. "What are you waiting for?"

I snap back to reality and take a step forward. "Good morning, Mr. Ryner."

He looks up at me and quickly wipes a tear from his eye. "Oh, hey." He smiles.

"How ya doing this morning?" I face toward the monitor to give him some privacy.

"Good. Just finished talking with some of my students. They wanted to make sure I was okay."

"You're a teacher? What grade?" I can't help but ask, even though I know I should keep my distance.

"The fifth grade. It's definitely a fun challenge."

"They must love you," I say.

"I love them too. They're a fun bunch." His eyes glisten as he talks about teaching. "Look at me, getting all soppy."

"No, not at all. I think it's cute how passionate you are about your job." My eyes shoot open as soon as the words leave my mouth, and I'm instantly filled with regret. My cheeks are quickly warming, as if I've been sitting in the sun for too long.

"Cute, huh?" He raises a thick brow with a charming TV smile that has my knees ready to give out. Why does he have to be so dangerously handsome?

"I'm sorry. I, uh, don't know why I said that. That was inappropriate." I shake my head in disbelief and quickly move on, hoping to put an end to this awful moment. "Uh, anyway... I just wanted to let you know my shift is over, so Alison will be here soon. Do you need anything before I go?"

"No, I'm okay," he says, charming smile still intact.

"Have a good day." I quickly turn away and speedwalk out of his room.

***

The house is empty by the time I get home. Aiden must have left for work early.

"Alexa, play music," I call out from the bathroom as I turn the shower to nearly the hottest setting. I toss my scrubs into the washer as I wait for the bath water to heat. This is my favorite part of the day.

It's important to remove any trace of the hospital from my body before getting into bed. I love my work, but the job leaves me feeling disgusting, with all the bodily fluids and such.

I step directly into the scorching rainfall, submerging my face and hair immediately. The hot water turns my skin bright pink as it burns away the grime and embarrassment of today.

Soap suds slide down my legs and float into the drain. That awkward moment with Henry has been nipping at me all morning, but I try my best to bury it in the back of my mind with the rest of my humiliations.

After blow drying my hair, I head to my pitch-black bedroom. Blackout curtains are well worth the price when you have my absurd sleep schedule. Besides, the Arizona sun is unforgiving to us nocturnal people.

I fall face down into my cold pillow. The bed welcomes me like a large cloud. I thought it would take longer for me to fall asleep, but I immediately feel darkness consume my mind and body, and the voice in my mind grows quieter as I drift away.

9

HENRY

SATURDAY, JUNE 17TH: 7:30 A.M.

She called me cute.

I'm watching her plump lips move as she speaks, and it looks like art. I wish I had the talent to paint her. Charlie's olive skin and dark eyes are warm and remind me of home. I immediately feel at ease around her.

"I'm sorry. I, uh, don't know why I said that. That was inappropriate." Her eyes grow wide in embarrassment. "Uh, anyway... I just wanted to let you know my shift is over, so Alison will be here soon. Do you need anything before I go?"

She seems to second-guess herself a lot. Why is she so nervous?

"No, I'm okay," I say.

She smiles in relief. I can tell she's trying to end the conversation so she can leave, but I selfishly want to ask her to stay. I don't know many people in Redwell, and it would be nice to have someone to talk to. I've only lived here for a year and I've been too focused on work to meet anyone.

Before I realize it, she's leaving the room. Her hair bounces as she walks, highlighting several shades of brown and gold.

"Have a good day." Her voice is as smooth as chocolate and leaves me wanting more.

"Bye, Charlie," I say quietly to myself.

What an odd week, I laugh.

My new nurse drops a tray of breakfast food on the table above my lap. There are French toast sticks, scrambled eggs, and a small bowl of soggy sliced fruit. The French toast is surprisingly delicious for hospital food, perfectly crispy on the outside and light and airy on the inside. I might actually ask for seconds. The scrambled eggs on the other hand are a different story and tastes like wet sawdust.

"Hey, Alison?" I ask my nurse before she walks out.

"Yes, hun?" She looks over.

"Do you know my overnight nurse, Charlie?" A smirk creeps onto her face as I ask.

"What about her?" She tilts her head down, peering at me above her thin glasses.

"Well, I think I should do something nice for her, since she's the one who saved me after my accident." I slide my fingers through my hair to hide my nervousness. "Maybe I can just send a thank you note or something to her workstation. Do you think you could help me with that? I know it's outside your job description." I try not to look too desperate. Although, I kind of am.

She lets out a loud laugh. The power in her chest shocks me at first. "Sure, I can do that." She smiles. "Let me know when you have something you want me to give her," she says as she walks away.

I can't help but smile too. Talking to a smart, sexy woman like Charlie almost makes getting hit by a car worth it.

10

CHARLIE

SUNDAY, JUNE 18TH: 5:45 P.M.

I DON'T KNOW what I'm doing back so soon. I'm pacing outside his hospital room, debating whether I want to go in.

After a few deep breaths, I decide to go for it. I knock two times before opening the door. "Henry?" I ask as I step into his room, quietly closing the door behind me.

"Hey there. You're back so soon?" He asks with a devious grin. "I'm glad."

"I figured you could use the company," I say as I inch closer to his bed.

"I brought you a green juice from downstairs. They're not the best, but they get the job done." I reach out to hand it to him.

"Thanks. This is actually one of my favorites." His large hand brushes against my fingers as he reaches for the cup. Electricity shoots through every cell of my body.

I get a better look at his face at this close distance. He truly is a beautiful specimen. His face is well sculpted, and he has a thick head of wavy brown hair. I wish I could run my fingers through it, but I resist.

"So, Charlie," he says.

I melt when he says my name. His voice is strong yet kind. "Yes?" I ask.

"Why are you really here?" His eyes grow darker as they concentrate on me. I can tell he's analyzing my movements.

"Uh, what do you mean? I-I work here," I stutter.

"You know what I mean," he says as he sits forward, inching closer to me.

I can't help but stand here, paralyzed, waiting to see what he does next.

He leans in closer and wraps his strong arm around my waist to pull me in. His hot breath on my chest has my body numb with excitement.

I look into his honey-brown eyes and place my hands on his jaw. I crawl into his hospital bed and sit on his lap, not breaking eye contact.

His hands drop onto my ass, and he squeezes firmly. My body burns for him. Without thinking, I push my lips against his. They're soft and taste like black coffee.

He digs his hands into my lower back, squeezing my body closer to his, forcing a soft yelp out of me. He bites my bottom lip before pushing my face away from his.

Did he change his mind?

He looks me in the eye with a blank gaze. "Wake up," he says in a serious tone.

"Huh?" I respond.

"Get up, Charlie."

"Charlie!" Aiden yells from the bedroom door.

"What the hell do you want?" I snap out of it. "Can't you see I'm trying to sleep?" I shout, desperately trying to return to my dream.

"Fine. Be late to work!" he grunts as he leaves the room.

Ugh, I'm not ready to get up yet. My dream was just getting good. I roll to my side and look at my phone. My alarm is on snooze, so I must have kept turning it off. Shit, it's 5:45 pm. I should be dressed already.

I peel my sweaty body off my bedsheets and walk to my closet, taking my sweet time getting dressed because I'm just not ready to go in. That felt like the quickest sleep of my life. Then again, it always feels like that. My work schedule quite literally goes against human nature.

Aiden is hunched over the kitchen stove, making himself some dinner.

"Thanks for waking me up," I say.

"Mhm," he hums without looking at me. I can tell he's irritated with me, but I don't bother figuring out why. It seems like he's always irritated these days, even before the incident.

I grab a variety of random snacks from the fridge and toss them into my lunch bag, careful not to bump into Aiden in our narrow kitchen. No way will I eat one of those awful hospital salads again.

"Okay, then. Bye," I say as I walk out the front door.

"Yup," he says as I shut the door behind me, eyes not leaving the steaming pan in front of him.

11

———

CHARLIE

SUNDAY, JUNE 18TH: 6:50 P.M.

I CAN'T HELP but replay my dream on the car ride to work. It felt so real. This isn't okay. I'm entering dangerous territory, fantasizing about Henry like this, but I don't understand why he's consuming my thoughts.

I wish I could talk to someone, but who? I'm living a lie; the only other person who knows the truth is Aiden, and I don't think he'd be happy to learn Henry is my patient.

I'm sure Sheila would love to talk about this with me. I just hate that I can't be fully honest with her. She's become one of my best friends since moving to Redwell—one of my only friends, actually. Forming friendships in adulthood is hard enough without the added pressure of my insane work schedule.

I toss my things in my locker and head to my section, finding Sheila leaning against the nurses' desk with a big smile. She beckons me with her head, bright eyes gleaming.

"What are you so giddy about?" I ask suspiciously—until a beautiful bouquet of flowers on the counter behind her catches my eye. "Ah, is that why?" I point to blue hydrangeas neatly

52

wrapped in an eggshell yellow tissue paper. "Did Shawn send them for you?"

"No." She lets out a long sigh and matches my facial expression, as if waiting to drop a bomb on me. "Why don't you check the note?"

Are these for me? Did Aiden send them as an apology? I suspiciously pull a folded piece of paper from a small, tiffany blue envelope tucked inside the ribbon. I can't remember the last time I got flowers, let alone ones like these. Aiden usually springs for the grocery store bouquet with the $12 price tag still attached, but I guess it makes sense that he went big, considering the circumstances.

I open the note.

Charlie,

I realized after you left that I didn't actually thank you for saving my life. Please forgive me. When you're not busy caring for your other patients, I would love to show my appreciation with some coffee. I'm still mostly confined to a hospital bed, but I can order delivery from any coffee shop you like.

See you soon,
Henry Ryner

My heart stops as I read his letter. Henry sent this to me? Why would he do that?

"That's some bouquet. Are they special occasion or apology flowers?" Sheila stares at me with wide eyes, biting her thin bottom lip in anticipation. "What does the note say?"

I'm still trying to process what I just read. I can't believe he sent me flowers. "Uh, they're from Henry," I say, voice just above a whisper. "He's just thanking me, that's all," I say nonchalantly, trying to quickly end the conversation.

"Henry?" Sheila's voice perks up.

"We can talk about it more tonight," I say with a look that says *please drop it*. I don't need these other nosy nurses listening in on our conversation. People are talking about me enough after the accident; I don't need to add fuel to the fire.

Obviously catching my drift, Sheila nods and walks away with a goofy grin.

I smile back and shove the folded note into my pocket as I head to my first patient's room. Why do I feel like this is more scandalous than it really is? That sex dream must be messing with my head. I do have a habit of blowing things out of proportion. *Focus, Charlie.*

I grab my patient's chart and try to redirect my attention. I need to focus on work right now. I can't let myself get distracted so easily. So what if a handsome man sent me a beautiful bouquet? Who cares if he wants to buy me coffee too? I nearly slap myself to get these thoughts out of my head.

"Are you okay?" the older woman in the bed before me asks.

"Aren't I supposed to be the one asking you that?" I cross my arms.

She laughs weakly at my response. "I suppose you're right. You just look like you have a lot on your mind," she says as she stares longingly out the window. "*Man* problems, I suppose?" She gives me a curious side eye. "Or *woman*? I know times are different now."

"More like *men* problems," I emphasize.

She laughs to herself as I check her blood pressure. "Men," she scoffs. "I've had my fair share of problems with them." She looks at me as I unwrap the Velcro cuff from her frail arm.

"Yeah? Care to share any wisdom?" I laugh.

"Hm. Men problems," she quietly repeats to herself. "Well," she says after thinking for a moment, "choose happiness over comfort. Had someone told me that when I was your age, maybe I wouldn't have trapped myself in a loveless marriage for so long." She gives me a soft smile and gently pats her warm, spotted hand on my arm.

I feel unsettled by her comments, like she peered deep into my soul and read me my fortune. Am I so visibly unhappy that even a stranger with cataracts notices?

She must sense the tension in my face. "But what do I know?" she roars. "I'm sorry for saying anything. It's really not my place. My daughters always tell me I meddle too much." She throws her hands in the air. "But I can't help it! It's one of the perks of being old." She closes her dreary eyes to get some rest, grin still intact.

"That's okay." I smile. "You're right, though. Thank you." I gently remove her hand and turn to leave.

Happiness over comfort, I repeat to myself. Am I happy right now, or have I been too comfortable to change things?

I know the answer, but I don't want to admit it. The truth is, I'm terrified of my life without Aiden. Not because I want to be with him, but because I don't know anything else. We've been together for so long, I can't imagine myself starting over alone.

The thought of calling off our engagement, breaking the news to our families and friends, and moving into my own place is terrifying. I can't say I haven't thought about it, though. I sometimes find myself looking at studio apartments on Zillow, just to see if I could afford it. Aiden makes more than me and pays a larger portion of our rent, so I would definitely need to downsize.

I feel like such a loser. I still have love for Aiden, so why am I allowing myself to be consumed by such negative thoughts?

I try my best to silence the debate in my head and get back to work.

12

CHARLIE

MONDAY, JUNE 19TH: 7:30 P.M.

I'M EVEN MORE nervous to see Henry than I was yesterday. He sent me flowers, expensive ones, and wants to buy me coffee? Is he flirting with me, or was that really just a 'thank you for saving my life' bouquet?

I catch myself picking the dry skin on my lip as I get closer to his room. It's a nasty habit Aiden is always trying to get me to kick. I can't help it, though; my fingers automatically do it when I'm stressed. It's gotten to the point where I don't stop until I taste blood.

My heart flutters as I reach for his door.

"Knock, knock." I smile from the doorway. "Can I come in?"

His partially drawn curtains expose the foot of his bed, where I can see his toes wiggling underneath his sheets like a giddy child.

"Oh, hey!" he says as I peek my face around the curtain.

"How are you feeling today?" I ask as I make my way to his monitor.

"Better than yesterday." He sighs as he stretches out his long arms. "How are you?"

"Oh, uh, better than yesterday." I smile back.

"Yeah? Did something happen?" he asks with a mischievous grin.

"Thank you for the flowers. They're beautiful." My smile fades. "I also saw your note. Please don't thank me. All I really did was call the police," I say toward the floor.

"No," he responds firmly, looking tenderly into my eyes. "The nurses told me you checked me out and stayed by my side until the police showed up. I was really lucky you were there."

I look at him for a moment and immediately get caught in his gaze, like some sort of honey trap. I feel helpless when our glances meet, as if he's cast a spell on me, peering into the deepest corners of my soul.

"I was just doing my job," I utter.

"Regardless of why you did it, I'm grateful," he says without looking away. His brown eyes are laced with gold, like streaks of sunlight in a dark cave.

Eye contact makes me feel vulnerable, so I turn away. I'm too ashamed to look him in the eye while he praises me as some false idol. "Well, I guess I was just in the right place at the right time."

How can I just lie like this? Is this my new thing? I'm taking credit for something I didn't do. I'm not a hero. I'm a criminal accomplice who belongs in jail.

"Charlie? Are you okay?" he asks, pulling me from my thoughts.

I perk up. "Oh, yeah. Sorry, I'm okay," I say with a fake smile. "I'm just tired."

"Right. Well, I promised you a coffee." He crosses his arms. "If you give me your order, it will probably get here by your next check-in." He runs his fingers through his scruff.

While I know I shouldn't be too friendly with Henry, there's just something about him that makes me want to let my guard down. My crippling anxiety around him is slowly waning.

"Okay, I guess a coffee wouldn't hurt. I'll take an americano please," I say.

"Coming right up," he says as he pulls out his phone.

"Okay then. I'm going to finish my rounds. Buzz me if you need anything." I catch myself rubbing his note between my fingertips as I walk toward the door, and I quickly slide my hand out of my back pocket.

Perfect. I look at myself in the mirror as I try to scrub my patient's vomit from my pants with a wet napkin and hand soap. Luckily, I keep an old pair of scrubs in my locker for occasions like this one. I toss my soiled clothes into a plastic bag and change into my slightly dingy but clean uniform. I swear I can still smell the puke on my body. I'm not even halfway through my shift, and I'm already over it.

Oh, well. Time to finish my rounds.

"Hello." I walk in to find the old woman from earlier sleeping peacefully in her bed.

She was supposed to be discharged this morning, but it looks like the doctor wants to keep her for another night of observation. I approach carefully, trying my best not to disturb her.

"Ms. Steward, I'm just going to check your blood pressure," I whisper as I gently wrap the thick belt around her dainty arm.

Her drooping face looks sad when she sleeps, completely different than the spunky woman I spoke to before. She talks about her daughters a lot; I hope they've paid her a visit. It saddens me to see the number of people who come in without any family members or friends to lean on.

Her heavy eyes shoot open in terror when I pull the Velcro

strips apart to unwrap the blood pressure belt. "Huh?" She gasps. "Oh, it's just you." She exhales in relief.

"I'm sorry to wake you. Are you feeling okay?" I ask.

"Um, I'm feeling alright. Still not using the bathroom," she groggily admits.

"Okay, no worries. I brought you some medicine to hopefully help with that, okay? Here you go." I place a large white pill in her crooked fingers and hand her a small plastic cup of water. Once she swallows it, I turn the lights back off.

"Okay, get some rest. Let me know if you need anything else," I say as I walk out of her room and on toward Henry's.

I knock loudly on his door before walking in, finding his face buried in a book.

"Hello." I smile.

He slams the book shut and lays it on his lap. "Ah, hello again." He grins. "As promised, coffee." He grabs a small cup from his bedside table and holds it out for me.

"Thank you so much," I groan. "You have no idea how much I needed this today."

I grab the cup from his hand, grazing his rough fingertips as I pull it away. The touch of his skin sends goosebumps across my body.

"Another busy day, huh?" he asks. The dark circles under his eyes tell me he isn't sleeping well.

I quickly look away toward his monitor. "Uh, yeah." I take a nervous sip of my now lukewarm coffee.

"Sorry if it's cold. It arrived a little bit ago, but I didn't want to call you over if it wasn't urgent." He rubs his arm awkwardly.

"I don't mind. Anything beats coffee from the break room." I take another sip then walk over to his bedside. His body jolts for a moment as I reach for his arm. "Sorry, I just want to check your IV site," I say.

"Oh, yeah, sure," he says.

"I'm going to close your IV line for now. This should make things a little more comfortable for you," I say, trying to ignore his body heat that's radiating into me.

"So, um, I need to admit something." He rubs his free hand on his leg as he works up the courage to finish his thought. "I didn't just send those flowers to thank you. The truth is, I also wanted a chance to talk to you again. Please, let me know if I'm overstepping. I can handle rejection." He laughs.

He wanted to talk to me? I look down at my bare left hand and feel grateful I don't wear my engagement ring to work. Am I a horrible person for thinking that?

"Well, I'm always open for conversation." I smile. "It's the least I can do, since you're confined to this room."

"I believe there's a silver lining in every situation." He raises an eyebrow.

I remember a time when I didn't feel so awkward around men. In college, I spoke and flirted freely with them, but right now, I'm carefully trying to not trip on my words.

"So, Henry," I start, "is there something specific you wanted to talk about?" I take a step back and lean against the countertop as I wait for his reply.

He pushes a button on his remote control that lifts his bed upright. "Well, Charlie."

My name rolling off his tongue sends shivers down my spine. His voice is deep and smooth.

"I'd like to know more about the woman who rescued me. What's your story?" He crosses his arms.

"Hmm..." I take a moment to think over my answer. It's hard to say, because my story isn't an interesting one. It's a tale as old as time: woman gets engaged to her college sweetheart, and they live a moderately-happily ever after.

"Well," I hesitate, "I moved here from California a few years ago with my fiancé and have been working here for about two years now." I try my best to smile, but I can see a hint of disappointment on his face. I feel gross admitting I'm in a relationship. Will he think I'm a bad person for flirting with him? If he doesn't, I can always tell him who put him in the hospital. That'll sway him.

"Your turn," I say.

He lets out a long sigh and rubs his hands together. "Well, I'm originally from New York City. It's my first year teaching at Redwell Elementary. I came here alone, unfortunately, but I've made a few friends." His face looks soft, eyes distant.

"So, you're engaged, huh?" He slaps his hands on his lap. "When's the big day?"

"Oh, well, we haven't set a date." I sigh—I've been dreading the question. "To be honest, I'm not sure if we'll ever set a date." I laugh a little too hard.

"Oh? Why is that?" He looks at me with curiosity in his eyes, a thick brow slightly raised.

"We just have a lot going on," I say as I rub my right arm. *A lot going on.* That's the excuse I've been giving to anyone who asks. I can't admit my fiancé is dragging his feet. Aiden has been full of empty promises ever since I said yes to that damn question, like he gave up on being a caring partner as soon as he realized I wasn't going anywhere.

13

HENRY

MONDAY, JUNE 19TH: 7:25 A.M.

IT SOUNDS like she's been frantically working, but her appearance screams leisure. Her hair is pulled back into an intentionally messy ponytail, her tan skin glistening, like she just went for a swim. She looks down as she fidgets with her fingers, showcasing her long black lashes.

I can tell she's nervous, that eye contact makes her jittery. She only holds my gaze for about two seconds before looking away, which is a shame; her eyes are beautiful. The reflection of the ceiling lights in her eyes remind me of stars in the dark desert sky.

Hearing she's engaged feels like a punch to the chest, but it sounds like there's trouble in paradise. Why else would she joke like that? *I'm not sure if we'll ever set a date.* That may be good news for me, though.

I'm infatuated with this woman, and if being her friend is the only way to see her, so be it. I just want to be close to her.

"Yeah, life has a habit of getting in the way," I respond.

"You enjoy reading?" she asks, pointing to the tattered book on my lap. "What's it about?"

I smile; it's actually one of my favorite books. "Um, it's a thriller about a serial killer targeting young women in the 80s. It's pretty good. Do you like to read?" I ask.

"I used to, but work got too busy. Now, I fall asleep as soon as I get home." She leans back against the counter. "But I would love to get back into it. It would just take the right book." She smiles as she tucks a loose strand of dark brown hair behind her ear.

I'm again taken aback by her beauty; even after working an overnight hospital shift, she's still radiant. I hate that she's engaged.

"What genres do you typically like?" I ask.

She scrunches her mouth and taps her fingers on the countertop behind her as she thinks. "I love crime and mystery novels, as well as the occasional romance." She blushes.

"I see," I say as I grab a paperback. *Withering Secrets*. "You should give this a try." I hold it out, hoping our hands meet again as she reaches for it.

Her eyes grow in surprise. "Oh no, I can't take that from you. What will you read?" She waves her hands, trying to reject my offer.

"A coworker is actually dropping off some books and paperwork for school tomorrow morning, so I'll have lots of material to go through." I smile.

This is the perfect excuse to see her again. *Please take me up on my offer*. I can tell she wants to. Hopefully, the chemistry I'm feeling isn't one-sided.

"Well, are you sure? I really don't know how quickly I can finish this. How will I give it back?" She hesitates; her eyebrows perch up when she's concerned. It's cute.

"How about this," I say as I grab a pen and notepad from my bedside table. "You can text me when you're ready to return it— or if you just have thoughts to share about the story." I slide a torn piece of paper into the book and slam it shut. "Here you go."

"Well, thank you." She smiles as she takes the book from my hand. "I should probably get going. My other patients are probably missing me. Thanks again for the coffee!" she says as she walks to the door.

"No problem. Let me know how you like it!" I shout as she leaves.

Her ass looks incredible in those scrubs as she walks away. It clings to her skin like silk, and for a moment, I imagine what she looks like underneath.

14

CHARLIE

TUESDAY, JUNE 20TH: 12:30 A.M.

I UNZIP my lunch bag and look at the pathetic meal. It looks like a nine-year-old packed it: carrot sticks, a pouch of apple sauce, animal cookies, a bag of turkey meat, and cherry tomatoes. I was in a rush, so I basically grabbed whatever snacks were available and threw them in my bag. It still beats that rotten salad I ate yesterday, though.

"How's it going?" Sheila enters the break room to make herself a cup of coffee. "You want one?" she asks, pointing to the single-serve coffee maker.

"Yeah, thanks. I can always go for a cup." I smile.

"So," she walks to me as the machine fills her paper cup, "are you going to tell me what the note said?" She raises an eyebrow and crosses her freckled arms.

I smile and pull the folded paper from my back pocket. It's warm, like paper straight from the printer. "Here you go."

A wide grin appears on her face as she unfolds the note.

I head to the coffee maker while she gathers her thoughts, replacing her cup with the 'I Hate Mondays' mug from the cabinet. I rinse it out first because the dishes in the break room never seem clean enough. Once my coffee is ready, I grab both of our cups and bring them to our table.

"So?" I ask.

"You must have made quite the impression," she says with a playful smile. "He wants to buy you coffee."

"Actually, he already did. He had it delivered and gave it to me earlier," I say as I shove an animal cookie in my mouth. Shelia briefly opens her mouth to speak before quickly squeezing her lips shut to force a stiff smile.

"You look like you want to say something." I refold the note and return it to my pocket.

"Well..." Her voice drifts off. She looks me in the eye, and I can tell she feels sorry for me. "Well, I guess there's no harm in just coffee."

"And..." I try to push her to finish her thought.

"I don't know. I'm just wondering what the point is. I mean, you're engaged, so why are you flirting with this guy?" She shrugs.

"Right," I sigh. "Aiden." I look down at the little black bubbles swirling around my mug and remember the man I promised to marry. When did life get so complicated?

"I was honest with him, you know. About being engaged. So I'm not misleading him," I try to justify.

"Well that's good." She drops the subject and takes a sip of her coffee, avoiding all eye contact with me.

Could she be right? Am I sending Henry the wrong signal? He's my patient, after all. It wasn't very professional of me to let him buy me a coffee.

I'm overthinking this. I'm not doing anything wrong here. Henry knows I'm in a relationship.

I wrap my hands around my warm mug and let the hot liquid warm my insides. This is the perfect pick-me-up for a cold hospital. The corner of Sheila's mouth curls downward, as if she has something else to say but is hesitant.

"What's the matter?" I ask. "You look like you have something you want to add."

"I don't know. I don't want you to get upset." She takes another sip of her coffee.

"I promise, I won't."

She looks around the room to check for eavesdroppers and takes a deep breath. "Okay, well, I just wonder why you're even with Aiden. It seems like he doesn't treat you well, and you never seem happy. Do you really think things will get better after you're married?" She looks deep into my eyes.

I'm stunned silent by the blunt honesty. I open my mouth to speak, but my words get caught in my throat.

"I'm sorry. Obviously, you know your relationship much better than I do," she apologizes. "I shouldn't have said anything."

"Really, it's not a big deal." I finally find my voice. "You know I don't have many people out here, so I really appreciate talking about this with you." I place my hand on hers. "You're right about all of it. Aiden and I do have issues, and I don't see them improving anytime soon," I sheepishly admit. "I know something has to change. I just don't know what to do about it yet."

"Just sleep on it. I'm sure you'll figure it out," she says warmly.

My watch interrupts our heart-to-heart to remind me to clock back in.

"Break time over." I force a smile as I close my lunch bag. "I hear what you're saying and will definitely think about it. Thanks for talking about this with me," I say as I stand.

"Anytime," she says as she goes in for another sip.

"Good morning. How are you feeling today?" I ask as I enter my next patient's room. I'm tired but happy—my shift is almost over.

"Good morning," a bright-eyed teen with braces responds. "I'm feeling better today, thanks."

I set her tray of food on the table above her lap. "Bon appetit." I smile. "Another nurse will visit you after breakfast."

"Aw, you're off now?" She gives a fake pout.

"Just about, but I'll see you again tonight. Have a good rest of your day!" I'm usually exhausted by the end of my shift, but I'm feeling unusually good right now as I walk out. Maybe it's all the caffeine?

I pass Sheila on my way to the locker room, and she just flashes me a sleepy smile. "Have a good day." She yawns.

"You too," I say on my way to the sinks to freshen up. I pull back my stray hair and examine my red puffy face in the mirror before rinsing it with cold water to cool down then toss on a light layer of mascara and lip gloss. This is as good as it's going to get. I check my smile in the mirror one more time before heading out.

15

CHARLIE

MONDAY, JUNE 19TH: 8:12 A.M.

THE HOUSE IS empty when I get home. I wonder if Aiden even noticed I was running late. I haven't gotten any texts from him, so it's safe to assume he didn't. To be fair, he was probably busy rushing to the office and assumed I was working overtime, which isn't unusual for me.

I toss my bag on the kitchen counter, and *Withering Secrets* by Lori F. Ryner slides out. The corners of the cover curl back; I can tell he's read this copy at least a dozen times. I wonder why he likes it so much? I guess I'll need to read it to find out.

That'll have to wait for the weekend. Tomorrow is the end of my workweek, and right now, I need sleep. My eyes are heavy, and I feel like I've had one too many tequila shots.

I wake up to the savory aroma of bacon. I squint open my left eye and grab my phone to check the time. 5:05 P.M. For the first time in a while, I actually feel well rested. I stretch out my arms and legs and roll up to sit.

I find Aiden standing over the stove in the kitchen. He's still in his work clothes, gray slacks and an untucked white button-up shirt. He turns back to me and smiles. "Good morning sunshine," he says cheerfully.

Well, well, doesn't he seem happy. Aiden is a serious person who usually carries a straight face. He doesn't smile often, but when he does, it's quite a sight. He's handsome, in a surfer-turned-corporate kind of way—sandy blond hair that sometimes dangles in his face, ocean blue eyes, and toned shoulders showing he works out.

"Good evening." I smile suspiciously. "You making breakfast?" I ask, peeking over his shoulder.

"Well, I figured it's been a while since we've eaten together, with our schedules being so crazy and all." He grabs two plates from the cupboard and starts serving up scrambled eggs and bacon, holding both plates on one arm like a waiter. What's gotten into him? I sit down cautiously at the counter, waiting to be served.

"Coffee?" he asks as he sets the plates down in front of me.

"Woah, yes please. I'm getting the full diner experience, huh?" I laugh as he pours fresh coffee into my favorite blue mug. He grabs his own glass of tea and takes a seat beside me.

The smell of bacon makes me realize how hungry I am. I shove a whole crispy strip in my mouth and take a big gulp of the molten black liquid.

"So, what's the occasion?" I ask, trying not to sound too suspicious of his sudden good mood.

"What? Can't a guy make his lady food just because?" He laughs without making eye contact.

I can't help but feel like he's hiding something from me, but I don't know what. Did something happen today? Did the police try contacting him? The little voice in my head spits one bad scenario after another, so I shove another piece of bacon into my mouth to silence it.

"If you say so." Bits of meat fly out of my mouth as I speak.

I take another gulp of coffee to help wash down the food. This feels so nice. Breakfast is my favorite meal of the day, though I don't have much time to enjoy it these days.

"How was work?" I ask, trying to make some conversation.

"It was good. I got invited to a happy hour tomorrow night." He clears his throat, as if choking on his own guilt. He takes a sip of his chamomile tea as he waits for my response.

Is he kidding right now? He's going to a fucking bar after what he just did? The audacity of this man! I clench my fingers on my lap to stop myself from slapping him.

"Happy hour? You're not actually thinking of going after what just happened, right? I would think you'd stop drinking altogether after that." I try to keep my voice down, but there's no hiding the aggression in my tone. My entire body is trembling with rage. Does he not care about what he did? What he did to Henry?

He sets his mug down and exhales. This must have been why he was trying to butter me up. He was hoping I'd just let him go to the bar with his friends.

"Charlie, this is with important people from work. I don't need to drink just because it's at a bar. And if I do, it'll just be one or two beers. Nothing serious." He waves his hands to tell me to calm down, but it only makes me angrier.

I take a deep breath before responding. "Aiden, you nearly killed someone with your car because you were driving drunk. Is it really that important that you go to this?" My eyes well up, and my throat tightens.

"Listen, I get why you're so nervous about this." He places his hand over mine. "But I'm going to go to this. It would be more suspicious if I didn't. Plus, I'm up for a big promotion at work, so it's important I get face time with the bosses." He looks confident in his words, just like he did when he said he was okay to drive that night. "I promise I won't drive myself home if I drink, okay?" He tucks a strand of hair behind my ear and flashes a sympathetic smile. I can tell he's trying to reassure me, but his eyes tell a different story. They look blank and careless.

"Okay," I say. My feelings are fucking hurt right now. I wish he would listen to me, but he couldn't care less about what I say. "That's fine." I grab my plate and walk it to the sink. A tear escapes, but I quickly wipe it away before Aiden sees. He'll just accuse me of trying to guilt him into staying, which will only cause another pointless argument.

"I love you, Char-Char. Thanks for understanding." He gives me a rushed peck on the cheek, his five o'clock shadow scratching my face as he pulls away. "I'm going to hop in the shower and get ready for bed. Have a good shift."

I hover over the kitchen sink, unphased by Aiden's attempt at affection. I'm locked in a daze, staring at the dirty dishes. Days-old food layer several plates and pans in the sink. That would usually make me angry, but not right now. Our conversation has left me feeling numb, hollow. The sound of our bedroom door slamming shut pulls me from my day dream.

I look around our messy kitchen and start collecting trash. Coffee grounds stain the white grout around our coffee maker. A framed photo of Aiden and I on my graduation trip to Las Vegas has a smudge on the glass. We looked so happy, with his arms wrapped lovingly around my waist. What happened to us? I ignore the spotty glass.

I open the trash can to discard the junk in my hands and nearly pass out. What the hell? I see a familiar pair of brown eyes peering at me from beneath a pile of old coffee grounds.

I gently lift the soggy newspaper from the bin and lay it on our countertop, carefully brushing away the brown debris, and find a photo of Henry on the front page of the The Daily Gazette

— Aiden's usual morning read. He couldn't have missed this headline so why didn't he tell me?

My mouth falls open as I scan the article.

Local Elementary School Teacher Struck in Hit-And-Run
A beloved elementary school teacher is recovering in the hospital after being struck in a hit-and-run. No arrests have been made, but an investigation is underway. Police ask anyone with information to come forward or call their non-emergency hotline.

The whole town reads this paper. That means everyone I know is talking about the crash.

I can't contain myself and fall to my knees, crying like I've never cried before. Hot tears stream down my face, soaking my neck and chest. I hug myself tightly as I bawl next to the trash can. What has my life become? When did everything become so messy? I wish more than anything my mother could be here, holding me in her arms, telling me I'll be okay. I fucking hate it here. I hate Arizona!

I roll onto my side and lie on the cold kitchen floor, ignoring the crumbs of old food next to my face. I slowly start to regain control of my lungs as my phone starts ringing. It's my last alarm going off, reminding me to go to work. It's my emergency alarm, meant to wake me up if I sleep in too late.

Perfect. I grab the counter and pull myself up. *Okay, Charlie. It's time to get your shit together and go to work.* I dry my face on my sleeves, grab my bag, and storm out the door.

16

AIDEN

TUESDAY, JUNE 20TH: 6:22 A.M.

I WAKE up to an empty bed—again. At this point, I'm more used to sleeping alone than with my fiancée. I won't lie, her odd hours have really changed our relationship. We used to wake up together and spend the first hour of our morning talking and joking around in bed. Now, we don't even do that on her days off; her sleep schedule is so out of whack, she wakes up well before I do. By the time I'm up, she's already done an hour of yoga, gone on a run, and caught up on local news. It makes me feel like a lazy piece of shit, that's for sure.

I pull myself from bed and quickly get ready for work, grabbing an untoasted bagel from the cabinet on the way out.

Today is an unusually busy day in the office. We have a meeting next week where each department head will need to convince the board not to cut their budget for the next fiscal year.

My role is to compile the numbers that prove our department's efforts have been beneficial to the company so my boss can request more money—or at the very least convince them not to cut our funding. That being said, my computer has been blowing up all week with emails and messages regarding the project. I'm just grateful I won't physically be in the boardroom when they present. I imagine the geezers on the board will choke on their coffee when they hear my supervisor's proposal.

I'm double checking my work when a message bubble from Lexi pops up in the lower right corner of my screen.

You going to happy hour tonight?

I lean back in my chair and exhale. My brain is so fried from today, I don't know how I'll manage to socialize. After taking a moment to calm my brain, I sit up and type my response.

Yeah, you?

Ellipses appear as she prepares her response.

Yeah. Hopefully, Brandon and Ernie don't drink too much this time. They get touchy when they're drunk. LOL

That's true. Brandon and Ernie are a couple of middle-aged guys who obviously peaked in high school and apparently never learned how to talk to women, which is ironic, since one of them is married and the other used to be. At last year's company Christmas party, Brandon definitely groped a woman's ass but disguised it as an accidental bump. I'm surprised he didn't get fired then and there. I guess that's a benefit of weekly golf trips with the higher-ups.

I think all old farts are like that. Tell ya what, just sit at my table. If one of them grabs your ass, I'll grab theirs and see how they like it.

I laugh at the thought of smacking Ernie's ass. His mustache would probably jump in surprise, like they do in those old cartoons.

Okay, we'll stick together tonight then. :)

She responds, but I don't bother writing back.

―――――

"Hey." Lexi smiles as she approaches my desk. "You almost ready to go?" she asks, tapping her neatly painted pink nails next to my mouse pad.

I look at the time and realize it's already a quarter past five. I guess I got so caught up in work, I forgot to clock out. "Uh, yeah. I'm ready," I say as I roll my chair out. I swipe my backpack off the floor and follow her to the elevator.

Lexi presses the button to the parking garage. The scent of her perfume fills the small space, and I wonder if her skin tastes as sweet as she smells.

"Some of us are going to be carpooling there if you want to ride with me. I told Merideth I would drive her there, since she normally walks to work," she says, unaware of the effect she has on me right now.

I'm about to say no when I remember I took my car to work. Maybe it would be a good idea to leave it here at the office and ride with her after all. I don't want to be the idiot who returns to the crime scene. Well, I guess it's not technically the scene of the crime, but better safe than sorry. "Yeah, I'll ride with you. Thanks," I say.

We jump in her car, and I'm immediately hit with floral car freshener. It takes me a minute to get used to it. I look around, surprised to see how clean the inside is. The floormats look like they're regularly vacuumed, and it's not littered with trash. She makes Charlie's car look like a dumpster fire.

"Merideth says she'll be down in a minute. She wanted to change her clothes real quick," she says as she buckles her seatbelt and adjusts the rearview mirror.

Awkward silence fills the cabin. I'm normally good at making conversation, but I've had too much on my mind lately. The tension in the air is almost palpable. I watch her from the corner of my eye and can tell she's just as uncomfortable as I am. She's looking down at her lap, rubbing the thin fabric of her blouse between her fingertips. Just as I open my mouth to say something, the back door swings open. *Thank God.*

"Ugh. Sorry about the wait, guys!" Meredith is out of breath as she slides into the back seat. "I wanted to change into something nice for tonight, so thanks for waiting." She rustles a little bit as she tries to get situated. Meredith sports a white button up shirt with a black skirt and matching heels instead of the gym teacher running shoes and work pants she usually sports. I'm shocked by the paleness of her legs.

"No problem." Lexi perks up as she pulls out of the parking garage. Several people left before us, so we'll see if anyone is already drunk when we get there. My money's on Brandon. The guy downs beer like I drink water.

I look down at my phone to see if I got any texts from Charlie. Nothing, but that's not unusual. She's probably still asleep. Today was her Friday, and she usually likes to sleep in on her weekends. I know she was pretty upset at me last night, but I pretended not to notice to avoid an argument. She doesn't trust me right now, but I am not my mistake. One screw up makes people forget about the million other things you did right. It's frustrating. I just hope I don't get home tonight to an angry Charlie. With all the stress of the accident and this project at work, the last thing I need is to get bitched at as soon as I walk through the door.

I shove my phone in my pocket and try to push the negative thoughts out of my head. I want to have fun tonight. No bad vibes.

17

CHARLIE

TUESDAY, JUNE 20TH: 6:45 P.M.

I WAKE up drenched in sweat, eyes sticky from crying. I know I had a bad dream, but I can't remember what it was about. My bedroom is pitch black, just the way I like it, with the faint glow of the kitchen lights leaking in from under the door. My stomach growls at me to get up.

I roll up to sit and stretch my arms high above my head. I head into the kitchen, looking for something to eat, but I'm disappointed with my options. Why do we only have healthy food in the house? I'm not the same person I was when I went grocery shopping last week.

I plop into my usual spot on the couch and scroll my food delivery app. I'm craving cream-cheese rangoons and orange chicken. Once I have my Chinese food ordered, I pour myself a glass of cold chardonnay and turn on the evening news. I'm so busy with work, it's easy to fall behind in current events. That's not a big deal to many people, but I like to stay in the know.

We have a local election coming up, so most news coverage has been focusing on that, which I guess is a good thing. I'm hoping our accident will get consumed by the background noise and fade away. I feel icky inside for even thinking that.

Poor Henry. He looked so sad and lonely in his hospital bed. He said he's from out of state, so it makes sense that he doesn't have many visitors. He's like me in that sense—a transplant—though my family is only a short flight away while his is on the other side of the country. I sound pathetic even comparing the two situations.

I snap out of my thoughts to find myself looking at my work bag lying on the kitchen counter. I walk over and pull the tattered book from the inside pocket. The distressed cover is a bright orange painting with red streaks. It looks like it could be an abstract image of a sunset. This definitely isn't something I would have picked out on my own, but maybe that's a good thing.

I pile my book, cellphone, bottle of wine, and half-full glass into my arms and waddle to the bathroom, where I can run a bubble bath. There's no point in sitting around sulking about Aiden's bad behavior.

I turn on my meditation playlist and pour my favorite lavender and rosemary bath salts into the hot water, immediately filling the room with a soothing fragrance. I inhale deeply, welcoming the therapeutic aroma into my lungs. My clothes fall to the floor, and I dip my toes into the sudsy bath, careful to enter the water slowly to not burn myself. The tension in my neck and shoulders melts away as soon as my body is fully submerged.

Finally, my mind goes silent as I let the infused bathwater work its magic, focusing on the sensation of the bubbles and hot water entering my every pore. I feel completely at peace for the first time since the accident.

The water feels so good, I almost forget I came in here to read. I pour a little more wine into my glass and set it on my bamboo bath tray alongside Henry's book, take a sip, and open to the first page.

18

———

AIDEN

TUESDAY, JUNE 20TH: 7:10 P.M.

IT FEELS STRANGE, coming back to this bar after what just happened. The pink lights and Hawaiian theme don't hold the same charm. It's like a good memory has been tainted, and I'm being forced to relive it.

Lexi returns to the table with two drinks and hands me one even though I told her I wasn't drinking tonight. "Here you go," she yells next to my ear over the live music.

"No thanks. I'm not drinking tonight, remember?" I shout back.

She points to her ears and smiles, pretending not to hear me. "Sorry, I can't understand you! Here, drink this." She shoves an ice cold copper mug into my hands. "You'll like it." She nods with a mischievous grin.

I hesitate for a moment but then remember I didn't drive myself here. *It's okay*. I'm an adult. I can drink if I want to. Plus, I can call a car to pick me up if I'm even a little bit tipsy.

"Okay." I raise my hands in surrender and grab the mug, cheers-ing with her and Merideth. The overpowering taste of vodka almost knocks me out of my seat. Is this girl trying to get

82

me drunk or what? I catch her and Merideth exchanging glances as I go in for another taste.

"How's it going over here at the kid's table?" Scott Richards, one of our supervisors, roars as he sets his heavy hand on my shoulder. Scott is a mountain of a man, but anyone who's met him knows he has a good heart.

"Hey, Aiden. Why don't we step out on the patio for a moment?" His voice turns more serious, and a feeling of uncertainty settles in the pit of my stomach as I follow him outside. I look back at Lexi as I walk away, and her bright blue eyes look nervous too.

"What's up?" I ask, trying not to sound too concerned.

"Look." He gets right to the point. "I was talking to the big guys about John's position today. I know they were initially leaning toward giving you the job once he left, but it looks like they're going in a different direction now. They're hiring outside the company."

I try to hide my disappointment, but I'm sure it's written all over my face.

"Aiden..." He pats me on the back with his book-sized hand. "Pick your head up, kid. I know this is disappointing, but you're young and talented, and I'm sure a better position will open up. I just wanted to let you know, because the guy they're considering is here tonight." *Ouch, that stings.* "I think he's the boss' nephew. He wants to introduce him to some of the other supervisors and see if he fits. So, play nice." He smacks the door and walks back inside. The loud music escapes for a moment and then goes back to a vibrating bass once the thick door swings shut.

Are they fucking serious? I work my ass off for this company, and they turn me down for a promotion for what? For some straight-out-of-college dumbass whose uncle runs the company? What the hell does he know? My knuckles are white from how tightly I'm clenching my fists. That fucking bastard. I kick the brick wall in frustration, stubbing an ingrown toenail that I didn't know I had. My rage intensifies like a pot of boiling water about to spill over.

Okay, calm down, I try to convince myself. *Don't let the others see you like this. Just go inside and act unbothered.* I'll show them they've made the wrong choice.

The patio door slowly creaks back open, almost hitting me during my internal pep talk.

"Are you okay?" Lexi rushes to my side. "What happened?" Worry is written all over her face.

"I guess I'm not getting John's spot. They're going with Gary's nephew," I spit. "And if that's not shitty enough, the kid's coming tonight so he can chat with Scott and the other supervisors." I look away so she can't see how upset I am.

She inches closer, rubbing my bicep. "I'm so sorry, Aiden. I can't believe they did that to you. And after all the hoops they made you jump through for that position too." She looks down in disappointment. "Come on. Let's go inside and get you a refill. The company's paying, so we might as well get their money's worth." She grabs my hand and pulls me back into the music. I swallow the rest of my now watered-down vodka in one gulp and follow her to the bar.

Sorry, Charlie. Looks like I'm having more than one drink tonight.

19

CHARLIE

TUESDAY, JUNE 20TH: 10:58 P.M.

IT'S BEEN a while since I've read a good book. I used to read a lot in high school and college, but I slowly stopped over time. It's been harder to find something that holds my attention when I can just relax and scroll through my phone instead. This is a good reset for me.

I get an alert on my phone telling me the food has arrived, which is perfect, because I'm officially starving, like a bear fresh from hibernation. I pull the drain and stand before wrapping myself in a fresh towel.

I gather my things and take them into the living room so I can continue reading before I run to the front door, peering through the peephole first to make sure the delivery person is gone. With food in hand, I plop myself onto the couch, towel and all, and dig in. This is the first decent meal I've had all week. I shove a piece of orange chicken in my mouth, followed by a fork full of chow mein.

I start thinking about the book Henry recommended. It's about a detective working to find a serial killer who has been terrorizing their city. I'm having enough anxiety as it is, trying to hide my involvement in a hit-and-run; I can't imagine what it would be like to be a serial killer.

I grab the book from the coffee table to look at the back cover, and the author's name catches my eye. Lori F. Ryner. It's a young woman with dark, shoulder-length hair, light eyes, and a bright smile. She's stunning. Could she be related to Henry? Is this why he's read it so many times? I flip to the front of the book to examine the cover again. I wonder who she is.

I set the book on the coffee table and pour myself another glass of wine. As I go in for a sip, I notice a piece of paper sticking out from the book's pages. I set my glass down and slide the paper out to examine it. Oh my gosh, how did I forget?

I open the folded piece of paper to see his name and phone number neatly printed. I carefully inspect the curves of his handwriting, tracing each line with my eyes.

Feeling buzzed and pretty courageous, I quickly type his number into my phone and start drafting a text message.

> Hey, it's Charlie. I've been reading your book and love it so far, but I have a question for you.

I stare at the screen as my finger hovers over the 'send' button. Should I do this? Hell yes, I should! I take another gulp of wine as I try to hype myself up before pressing the button. I squeal in excitement and lie down. I'm too nervous to think. What will he say? What will he think? Oh no! What time is it?

I grab my phone and see that it's 11 P.M. Will he think it's weird I'm texting him so late? I panic and hit send before dropping my phone and turning up the TV. Hopefully, the laugh track will drown out the cries in my mind.

I curl up in a ball on the couch, trying my best to calm my thoughts, when I see a soft glow from the corner of my eye. My heart starts beating so hard, it feels like I'm about to go into cardiac arrest. I grab my phone, almost too scared to look, and open the notification.

Oh, it's Aiden. I roll my eyes. I don't want to admit how disappointed I am.

> I had a couple of drinks, but it's fine. A coworker will take me home. Gn.

Now I'm more disappointed. I knew he wouldn't stick with his 'one or two drinks' promise. At least he's not driving himself home this time, so that's already some progress on his part. I don't even bother responding.

My eyes are getting heavy. The wine and food are making me tired, and it's not even midnight. I close my eyes for a moment and let the food coma take me.

Laughter pulls me from my deep sleep. I can tell several episodes have passed since I dozed off. It's okay, though; I've seen this show several times. I grab my phone to check the time and see I missed a text from Henry.

I jump up and rub my eyes. I try reading his message, but my vision is still blurry from sleeping face down on the cushion. I run to the kitchen and rinse my face with cold water. It's electrifying, and I'm immediately buzzing with energy.

> Hey, It's good to hear from you. Ask away.

> Are you related to the author?

He responds quickly.

> Sharp eye. The author is actually my mom, which is why I love it so much. How are you liking it so far? Don't let my bias sway you.

I belly-flop back onto the couch, my legs swinging up behind me like a giddy schoolgirl on the phone with her crush. I stare at his message, wondering if I should respond tonight or wait for the morning. He's probably asleep; I wouldn't want to wake him. Then again, he knows I work the overnight shift, so it would make sense for me to be up right now.

I stop overthinking and decide to just text back.

> I like it! It's been a while since I've gotten into a good story. Did she write any other books?

I'm looking for any reason to keep talking to him.

I just realized it's two in the morning, and I don't see any sign of Aiden. Did he come home while I was napping? I open our bedroom door to find our empty, disheveled bed. It's a weeknight; where is he?

I text him, really hoping he's not doing anything stupid.

> When are you coming home? Don't you have work tomorrow?

20

AIDEN

WEDNESDAY, JUNE 21ST: 2:15 A.M.

AND THEN THERE WERE THREE.

Most of the office is gone now, save for Lexi, the boss' nephew—Marshal—and me. Meredith ordered a ride home a while ago. Why the hell is this guy still here? We're sitting on the patio, enjoying the cool breeze. Lexi's been so consumed in her conversation with this guy, they've both completely forgotten about my existence. Is this what it's going to be like in the office from now on?

I grab my phone to check the time when I see a text from Charlie. *Shit.* I stand and stretch my arms. "I should probably get going," I announce.

Lexi's eyes get big, as if she just realized I was here. "Oh no, you're leaving? Wait, I drove you. Let me get my keys." She starts rummaging through her bag.

"No, it's okay. I can just order a ride."

"No, no, no," she says into her purse. "I've only had one drink, so let me take you home." She smiles. "It was nice meeting you, Marshal. I guess I'll see you around the office." She stands gracefully and walks back into the bar. I can't help but smile at the disappointed look on his face.

89

"Nice meeting you, bro." I follow her inside without waiting for his response.

Lexi's skin-tight pink skirt slowly crawls up her ass as she walks to the car, prompting her to pull it down every few seconds. Her skin looks enchanting under the purple fluorescent bar sign, almost like some sort of magical pixie. It makes me grateful she chose this outfit for tonight.

"Thanks for driving me home, Lexi. It's not far from here," I say as I slide into the passenger seat.

"No problem." She tucks her hair behind her ear. "You can direct me," she says as she starts the engine. She buckles up and sits back in her seat. "I'm just waiting for the engine to warm up." She laughs nervously. "So, what did you think about Marshal?" she asks to fill the silence. I hate the sound of his name leaving her lips.

"Eh, he seems like a poser to me. Definitely not qualified for the job." I fold my arms in disgust, still bitter about the whole thing. "But, uh, it seems like you two hit it off," I suggest, looking for any clue she's interested in him.

"Oh yeah, he seems nice. A little too flirty, though," she admits.

"Yeah, I noticed that." I try not to sound jealous. "But it kind of looked like you were flirting with him too."

"Oh really? No, not at all!" she says defensively. "I definitely wouldn't want anyone thinking that."

"Oh yeah? Why's that? He too ugly for you?" I joke, poking her shoulder.

"No, it's not that. It would just look, uh, unprofessional. That's all," she stutters. "Anyway..." She changes the subject as she puts the car in drive. "Where to?"

"Uh, just turn right out of here and go straight for about a mile," I say.

I examine her side profile from the corner of my eye. Her

face is stunning. Her cheeks and lips look rosy from sitting outside in the cold for so long. The top of her breasts peak out of her low cut blouse, slightly bouncing with each bump in the road.

I lay my face against the cold glass to distract myself, watching as the tall cacti and street lamps pass us by.

"I'm sorry they passed you up for the job. Hopefully, something else will open for you soon." She gently lays her right hand on my shoulder. The smell of her skin is sweet and intoxicating.

"Thanks. I'm sorry for being such a bummer. You're always so nice to me. I really don't deserve it," I say, keeping my eyes locked on the road. I'm feeling too vulnerable and embarrassed to look at her as I say it. I can't stand when someone feels sorry for me, but I can't help but tell her how I'm feeling.

"Hey. You have every right to be upset." She returns her hand to the steering wheel. "And you're not a bummer. You make coming to work fun! Things would be so dull without you," she says. I can hear a smile in her voice as she speaks.

Her kind words warm me up inside. It feels nice to finally be appreciated by someone. "Gosh, you're making me blush," I joke. "But seriously, Lexi, thanks. You make work fun too. You're always so happy, it's contagious." This time, I look at her as I speak. "You're an amazing woman." I can't help but smile.

The car comes to a slow stop as we approach a red light. The street is empty and soaked in the soft orange glow of street lamps. Lexi turns to me with sad eyes. Did I say something wrong?

She pulls her parking brake and leans into me. Without thinking, I lean in too. She wraps

her dainty hands around my head and guides my lips into hers, gently stroking the inside of my lips with her tongue and laying one more wet peck on my mouth before pulling away. "I think you're amazing too, Aiden." She smiles.

I grab her face and pull her back in for more. I can't control myself. I need to taste her, to feel her. I'm like a child enjoying a slice of chocolate cake for the first time; I can't help but dig in now that I've had a taste.

One of her hands grabs my inner thigh, rubbing while the other strokes the side of my face. My jeans tighten as her hand moves up my leg.

A loud car horn blares from behind us, and we both jump in our seats. We got so caught up, we forgot we were still stopped in the middle of the street.

"Green means go, asshole!" a man yells as his car screeches past us.

Lexi quickly returns her hands to the steering wheel. "Oh my God, I'm so sorry," she apologizes as she puts the car back into drive. "Uh, where do I turn?".

I'm still shaken by what just happened. "Uh, up ahead," I stutter. "Turn right after that playground." I point. "Then immediately go left. I'm at the end of the cul-de-sac." I lick the sweet taste of her gloss off my lips.

I sit still, in complete silence, as she pulls up to my house. I don't know what to say. *Say something, dammit. Anything!*

She stops at the end of our driveway, behind Charlie's beaten up hatchback. "Aiden, I'm so sorry," she says. "I know I shouldn't have done that, but you're just so special, and I got caught up in the moment. I really hope I didn't ruin things between us." She looks down at her lap in shame.

I struggle to find the words to respond, but I'm at a loss. I wish I could tell her the truth—how much that kiss meant to me, how I didn't want to stop—but I resist. "Thanks for driving me home, Lexi. I had a good time." Disappointment washes over her face, as if she was expecting me to say something else. I open my door anyway. "Goodnight. I'll see you tomorrow. Please text me when you get home so I know you got there safe."

I close the door and try my best to smile for her sake. It took everything in me not to kiss her again right here, in front of my house.

It's been a long night. I'm tired and confused and need to go to bed. This is all too much.

21

CHARLIE

WEDNESDAY, JUNE 21ST: 3:02 A.M.

BRIGHT LIGHT SHINES through the cracks of our kitchen blinds as a car pulls up to the house. Aiden better have kept his promise to not drive himself home.

I run up to the window above the sink and peek through the plastic shades. It looks like he's sitting in a car with a woman, and they're deep in conversation. Who is she? What are they talking about? She doesn't look like the driver of a ride sharing app.

He steps out of the car and waves her off, waiting for her to turn out of sight before walking toward the house.

I sprint back into the living room and dive onto the couch when I hear keys jingling in the door lock. "Hey," I say, out of breath, as Aiden opens the door. "How'd it go?"

He looks concerned, eyes distant, as if he's just been told his grandmother died. He's probably expecting me to yell at him for staying out so late, but I don't. There's no point, and he's probably too tired and drunk to hold a meaningful conversation anyway. I'll save it for later, when we're both in a better headspace to talk.

"Hey," he says in a raspy voice. "It went okay." He clears his throat. "I didn't get the promotion. They're bringing in one of my boss' nephews instead," he says as he sets his coat, backpack, and keys on the kitchen counter.

"Oh, wow. That really sucks. I'm sorry. How'd you get home?" I try my best to sound casual.

He stops in his tracks as he thinks of an answer. "Oh, uh, a coworker dropped me off," he says. "I'm really tired, and it's been a weird day. I'm going to bed. Night." He starts undressing as he trudges into the bedroom, leaving a trail of clothing behind him.

I would have liked to know more, but it doesn't look like he's going to talk. I wonder why he left out being taken home by a woman? Maybe I'm just overthinking it, I convince myself.

I grab the book off the coffee table to pick up where I left off. It's just getting interesting. The story follows a female detective who's trying to solve the murder of a young woman, only to learn she's just one of several victims. She's a single mom on the force, trying to catch a serial killer who's targeting women who coincidentally resemble her teenage daughter.

My phone vibrates, and a message from Henry pops up. What's he doing up at this time?

> Yeah, that book is actually the first of a four-part series. It was pretty popular in the early 2000s. Glad you like it.

His mom is a famous author, huh? It's obvious now she took some inspiration from her personal life as she wrote this. I'm curious to know more about her. I imagine she's a firm yet gentle woman, patient and inspiring, just like the character in her book. It reminds me of my mom too. Maybe that's why her readers related to it so much.

> What are you doing up right now? I thought you would be asleep.

I guess sleeping can't be that comfortable in his condition. If I were him, I would want nothing more than to lay in my own bed.

> The beds here suck, and I can't get my leg comfortable. It's definitely going to take time getting used to. Are you usually up at this time?

> Yeah, my internal clock is wired to keep me up, even on my nights off. I kind of like it this way, though.

I text back immediately.

> Yeah? Why is that?

He responds just as fast.

> I just feel more productive at night. Plus, the Arizona heat is gross.

> I get it. I'm from NY, remember? I miss having more than one season.

Look at us. Already talking about the weather. I don't know why I'm smiling right now, but I can't help it. The image of him on that hiking trail with that dog pops back into my mind. Hot weather suits him.

> Why did you leave New York? That seems like a cool place to live.

I imagine him living in a chic industrial loft with exposed

brick and black, metal-lined windows. His place would be taste-fully decorated, with colorful bohemian rugs, a leather couch, and dozens of books. The room would smell like cigars and cinnamon.

> I guess I just wanted to get away from home for a bit. When I came across this position, it looked like a good opportunity. Plus, the city is really expensive, and teachers aren't treated well. Wby? Why here?

Get away from home? I wonder what happened, but I don't want to pry.

> To be honest, my story isn't interesting. I came here for school and found a great job after graduating. I'm originally from San Diego.

I feel kind of embarrassed about my life. I had an ordinary upbringing, no drama, no big life lessons. That transferred into adulthood, and I feel like something is missing because of it.

> So, are you a writer too?

I send a follow-up message, trying to take the focus off me.

The three dots appear on my screen and then disappear. The thought bubble pops up a couple more times and then goes blank. Did I hit a sore spot?

> I'm not published like my mother, but I write short stories. She's actually the one who inspired me to teach.

A little part of me melts. A handsome, fit, creative man who's good with children? *God help me.* Nausea hits as I remember

Aiden is sleeping in the room behind me. Should I really be texting Henry while I'm engaged?

Relax, I try to assure myself. Henry understands I'm engaged, so it's not like I'm leading him on or anything. It's just nice to have someone to talk to. I'm usually alone on my days off, since my sleep schedule is so different.

I decide it's best to end this conversation for now and plug in my phone to charge. I don't want to get distracted if he texts back. I'm afraid I'm crossing a boundary that's not meant to be crossed, but I can't help it. I feel inexplicably drawn to Henry.

22

HENRY

WEDNESDAY, JUNE 21ST: 8:30 A.M.

"GOOD MORNING," a nurse says as she walks into the room. "How are you feeling today?"

"Not bad," I respond. "Head still feels funny, but it's not hurting."

"Yeah, that makes sense. Concussion symptoms can linger for a couple weeks. You may still feel off even after you go home," she says as she checks my blood pressure. "Just try to avoid looking at your phone, okay? You need to rest that brain of yours."

"Yeah, I'll do that. Thanks," I lie.

My cell phone rings as she walks toward the door, and she turns to give me that 'don't even think about it' glare.

I laugh. "I know, I know. I'm not looking at the screen," I say as I press the answer button.

"Hello?" I answer as the nurse continues with her task.

"Hi, is this Henry?" an unfamiliar woman asks on the other side.

"Um, yes. Who is this?"

"My name is Muriel Smith, and I'm calling on behalf of mayoral candidate John Whitman. He heard about your accident and felt inclined to connect. We were wondering if he could visit you at the hospital to talk about your situation. Would that be okay with you, Henry?"

She asks the question like it's a formality, like she already knows the answer will be yes. What in the world could a guy like John Whitman want with me?

"What do you mean?" I ask, suspicious. "Why does he want to meet and talk about my accident?"

"Well, Mr. Whitman is a supporter of educators and would like to help share your story. We feel awful about what happened and would like to use our platform to bring aware-ness to your case. I understand the police still have no leads, correct?"

She has a good point. So far, the cops haven't found anything, but that's not very surprising, since it's a non-fatal hit-and-run. They probably have more important cases on their plates.

"I appreciate you reaching out, and while it would be good to get more eyes on it, I'm not really interested in you sensational-izing my story to get support for your campaign. I'm assuming that's why you're reaching out. Yes?" I clarify.

The woman holds her breath, as if the words got trapped in her mouth at the last second. "Well, we see this opportunity as a win-win for everyone. We can help bring attention that will pressure the department to prioritize your file. We genuinely care about and sympathize with your predicament. So, what do you say? Could we set up a time for Mr. Whitman to visit?"

"Thanks, but I'll need to think about it," I hesitate.

"Sure, I understand. Thank you for your time. Have a good day." The line goes dead.

That was strange. How did they get my phone number?

It could be good to talk with someone who can share my story and ask the community for any leads, but then again, I don't want to be a pawn in some political game. I don't know anything about this guy, and he wants me to be a poster child for his generosity. What if he turns out to be a whack job or pervert? I'll be guilty by association.

I would also hate for them to turn this into some sob story for the broken teacher. We know they will make this more dramatic than it needs to be to make him look like a hero.

I wish I could talk to my mom, but I don't want her to know I got hurt. She's got enough on her plate.

I lay my head back and close my eyes, trying my best to center myself. I need to clear my mind before making any big decisions.

CHARLIE

WEDNESDAY, JUNE 21ST: 6:10 P.M.

I WAKE up to the sound of buzzing and assume my phone is blowing up—but my screen is empty.

So...not my phone.

I roll out of bed and follow the loud sounds into the bathroom. The cellphone's vibrations echo on the countertop, amplifying the volume. It's Aiden's phone.

I look at the screen and see a chain of texts from someone named Lexi. Could this be the girl from the car? I quietly close the bathroom door behind me and lock it before opening his phone. I don't want him to see his messages have been opened, so I pull down the notifications tab and read the message preview.

> Are you okay? Is there any way we can grab some coffee or something to talk about what happened?

I can't read any of the others. What the heck is she talking about? Did something happen at the bar?

I'm staring at the message when the bathroom door handle starts shaking. "Huh? Charlie, can I come in? Why is the door locked?" Aiden asks as he continues to fidget with the door knob.

I jump in surprise and carefully put his phone back where I found it. "Yeah, just one second," I shout. "I just woke up and had to pee." I flush the toilet, unlock the door, and begin washing my hands.

"What's up?" I ask as he enters.

He looks around the room suspiciously. "Nothing. I was just looking for my phone," he says as he grabs it off the counter.

"Oh, okay," I respond.

"So," I follow him into the kitchen, "we didn't really get a chance to talk last night. How did it go?" I ask as I take a seat at the bar top.

He raises his eyebrow at me as he pours himself a glass of water. "It didn't go well, remember? I told you I didn't get the job." He continues staring at me, as if to see if I'm unwell.

"Oh, right. I'm sorry about that. Did anything else interesting happen?" I start flipping through a magazine to avoid eye contact, though I see concern grow on his face in my peripheral.

"Um, not really. The rest of the night was okay. I got to hang out with coworkers and shoot the shit. Regular stuff, ya know?" He finishes his drink in two gulps and walks away to avoid more questions.

I'm curious about this Lexi girl. Why hasn't he mentioned her before? Is she really just a coworker, or is she something else? I want to ask him point blank, but I don't think he would tell me the full truth. I guess I'll need to do some snooping when he goes to sleep tonight.

The deep rattling of Aiden's snores tell me it's the perfect time to start my investigation. There's no waking him up now.

I slowly unzip his work bag on the kitchen counter and slide out his laptop. It's connected to his cell phone, so I should be able to read his messages through this. I walk over to the couch and prop the computer open in my lap.

Here we go.

I tap the message icon at the bottom of the screen and see his conversation with Lexi at the top. I scroll to the beginning of the conversation so I can get the full scope of their relationship.

> Hey, you almost ready to clock out?

Lexi sent it right before he left the office yesterday, so it doesn't look like they text often. He didn't even reply. She then sent him several messages a few hours ago, while I was in bed.

> Hey, Aiden. I really wanted to say I'm sorry for last night. I don't want to lose you or ruin our friendship.

What is she apologizing for?

> You don't have to apologize. I could have stopped it, but I didn't, so it's not just your fault. It probably shouldn't happen again, though, as much as I want to.

She followed up with a request.

> Can we meet for coffee or something?

Okay, so Aiden definitely left some things out of his story. Something obviously happened between the two of them. Did they hook up? Why else would they be talking like this? I could try confronting Aiden, but I know he wouldn't be honest with me. Plus, he would only make me the bad guy for invading his privacy. He's had all day to tell me the truth, and he obviously chose not to.

Instead, I decide to ask the woman herself. I copy down her phone number and type it into my phone, quickly typing a text message before I have a chance to rethink my decision.

> Hi, Lexi. This is Charlie, Aiden's fiancée. I saw you two together yesterday and was hoping to ask you something woman to woman… Did something happen between the two of you last night?

Who knows if she's even awake, but I need clarity on the situation right now. I feel like our relationship has been broken for so long, and this would just be the confirmation I need.

She texts back almost immediately.

> I'm really sorry. I don't want to cause anything. I think you should talk with Aiden about it.

I type hastily.

> He'll just deny anything happened. Please. I deserve to know.

I see she read my message almost as soon as I sent it but isn't typing anything. I'm feeling nervous now, and I'm not sure why. A small part of me hopes they did something so I can use it as a reason to leave. But what if it was something completely different than what I'm thinking? Am I really willing to stay in an unhappy relationship?

> I kissed Aiden in the car on the drive home last night. It was my mistake, not his. I'm really sorry.

She's trying to take all the blame for this, but based on their conversation this morning, Aiden was also into it. This is all the confirmation I need.

I don't even bother texting her back. Uncertainty brews in my stomach as I realize I've reached the end of our relationship. I'm looking at her message confirming my suspicions, yet I'm not feeling angry, upset, or jealous. I'm not really feeling anything at all—just emptiness. I don't know much about marriage, but I know you're supposed to care more about losing them than this.

A single teardrop falls from my eye and lands on the keyboard of his laptop. I'm not sure why I'm crying right now. Frustration? Disappointment? Fear? I guess it's a combination.

I shut his laptop and slide it back into his bag, carefully zipping it closed. I feel empty inside, like I'm watching the final episode of a TV series I've invested so much time into.

I'm not sure who I am without Aiden. We spent our entire adult lives together. It's all I know. Still, I just can't keep pretending to be happy when I'm not. It's not fair to either of us.

I return to my seat on the couch and close my eyes, trying to focus on the sensations around me. It's a coping technique my therapist taught me in high school called grounding. I sigh as I tilt my face up toward the ceiling fan. The blades are spinning erratically, rocking its base like a ship on rough waters. The wind feels cool and refreshing on my warm skin. I exhale and come to a conclusion: it's time to break up with Aiden.

How do I do that? How do I do this with him? He's not just some short-term boyfriend or a summer fling. He's the man I thought I would marry, who my family thought I would marry.

I need some fresh air.

My backyard is dark, with only the moon and stars offering enough light to see. I sit down on our dusty patio swing, trying not to be bothered by the scratchy, sun-damaged seat cushions I got at a garage sale.

While I'm not the biggest fan of the desert, the star gazing here is on another level. Thousands of twinkling lights glimmer above me like some sort of festival. This is where I like to come when I'm feeling overwhelmed and need to think.

An icy breeze nips at my nose and cheeks, creating a nostalgic feeling in my chest. I'm so in love with this atmosphere —the bright moon in the sky, the dark cutouts of the mountains, the whistling of the wind. The cold air is shocking to my body yet comforting, like the first jump into a swimming pool. I feel myself gaining a new sense of peace and clarity, like I finally know what direction I want my life to go in.

I pull out my cell and text Henry.

> Hey, how are you feeling?

It's only 10 P.M., so I hope he's still awake.
He responds quickly.

> Hey. I'm not too bad. Hby?

I try to imagine what he looks like in bed right now. Does he have bedhead? A five o'clock shadow?

> I'm okay. I'm just sitting outside star gazing. It's beautiful out right now.

> By yourself? Where's your fiancé?

I wonder if it bothers him that I'm with Aiden. Would he be relieved to know I plan on breaking up with him? I wish I could tell him it's already over, but I resist. Aiden should be the first to know.

> It's complicated right now, so I'm out here alone, just thinking about the meaning of life. lol.

hope that didn't sound too deep or desperate.

> Oh? Have you come up with any interesting ideas yet?

> I'm on the brink of a breakthrough.

> I'm actually not supposed to be texting right now because of my concussion, so I've been using voice to text. Would you mind if I called you? Something interesting happened today, and I'd like to talk it over with someone.

My stomach falls to the floor when I read that message. A call? I bolt into the kitchen and pour myself a glass of water. I hate my phone voice and have been told I sound like a child. I chug the water and go back outside, where Aiden won't hear me.

"Hey," a deep voice answers.

"Hey." I nervously clear my throat.

"How are you?" His voice is firm but calm, some concern in his tone.

"Oh, I'm okay. Thanks," I respond. It feels so strange to have a man genuinely interested in my feelings.

"So, I got an interesting call today from someone who said they work for John Whitman. Have you heard of him?"

Why does that name sound familiar? Does he work in the medical field? "Um, I'm not sure. The name sounds familiar, though. Who is he?"

"He's running for Mayor. I guess he wants to meet with me to talk about my accident," he says.

I feel the air get sucked from my lungs. "Oh?" Shivers run

down my spine. Now I remember. I saw him in a recent news report covering a local political debate. "Did he tell you why?" I follow up, trying to hide my worry.

I gasp for air, realizing I've been holding my breath this entire conversation.

"Um, well, it sounds like they want to share my story with the news or something to help get new leads. The police still don't have a suspect, so they think someone from the public might come forward with new information."

"Oh," I say unenthusiastically. "Uh, well, that's great news! Are you going to do it?" I try to change my tone.

"Um, I'm not sure yet, to be honest. I know this could be helpful, but at the same time, I don't want to be used to get someone more votes, especially if I don't know the guy or what he's about. Ya know?"

"Yeah, I get it. I would be hesitant to do that too, but you should do what you feel is best. I'm sure the police are working hard to find the person who did this to you. And the situation could be worse. Just try to look at the bright side." Selfishly, I want Henry to avoid this guy at all costs, but I don't want to persuade him one way or the other.

I pull up Henry's Instagram so I can look at photos of him while he talks, and I open the picture of him hiking. His tan legs are fit, with a large, abstract tattoo on his left thigh. He's too far from the camera for me to tell what it is. I imagine what it would be like to examine it up close.

"Yeah, you're right," he interrupts my thoughts. "I'm definitely going to think about it. So, how are the stars? See any UFOs yet?" He laughs.

"Not yet. I'm hoping soon, though." I giggle. "Maybe they can take me away from this place." I cringe at my own corniness.

Henry's breath goes silent. "So, uh, if you don't mind me asking; what's going on with you and your man?"

His straightforwardness takes me by surprise. "Oh," I utter. "Well, to be honest, it's not working. So I guess it's not that complicated." I laugh nervously before getting serious. "Things haven't been good for a long time now, and I think we're both just over it. I feel like we've only stayed together because it's been so long and that's what our families expect. Neither of us is happy." God, I must sound so pathetic. "Sorry to unload on you like that."

"No worries. Tell me then, what would make you happy?" he asks.

His question repeats in my mind. What would make me happy? I'm not sure what to say. "To be honest, I haven't thought about it much. I feel like I've fallen into a routine with someone who's more like a roommate. All I know is that right now, this isn't what I want. Maybe once I change that, I'll figure out what makes me happy." I exhale. "What about you, *Henry*?" I emphasize his name. "What would make you happy?"

"Hmm." His voice is smooth like butter. "Well, my job, for one. I love being a teacher. I also love reading, writing, and going outside. I try my best to only do things that bring me joy," he says. "Like talking to you."

I can feel his smile through the phone. "I enjoy talking to you too." I giggle. "You're an interesting person," I say coolly. "Do you know how much longer you'll be in the hospital?"

"Well, the doctor said my concussion symptoms improved and finally approved me for surgery, so it looks like I'll get my leg fixed in the next day or so. Hopefully, I won't be here much longer than that, because I'm ready to go home and sleep in my own bed again."

I'm curious to know what his home here looks like. Is it clean? Messy? Does he barely have any furniture?

"Surgery, huh? You won't be able to eat for eight hours before it, so tomorrow will be your last chance to eat a decent meal. What kind of food do you like?"

"Oh, are you trying to bring me something?" He laughs.

"Well, I work tomorrow, so I can bring you dinner on my way in...if you want. What would you like?" I have no idea where this idea came from, but I couldn't stop the words from coming out of my mouth. I just want to take care of him so badly.

"Haha, thanks." He yawns. "That's really sweet. I'm not picky, so I guess whatever you're craving for your break." His voice trails off.

"I guess burritos sound pretty good," I say, but he gives no response. "Does that sound okay to you?" I follow up.

I listen in for a response, but I only hear the faint sound of snoring. He must have fallen asleep. I burst out laughing and set the phone on my lap, careful not to hang up so I can listen to him breathe. I lean back on the bench swing and look up at the stars.

There's a feeling inside me that hasn't appeared in years, and it's *exhilarating*.

24

CHARLIE

THURSDAY, JUNE 22ND: 4:25 P.M.

I OPEN my eyes to the ceiling fan spinning chaotically above me. I don't remember turning that on when I went to bed, but now, my throat burns.

I roll to my side to check the time. It's earlier than I usually wake up, but I can't fall back asleep now. My eyes wander the room as I recall my conversation with Henry.

The butterflies in my stomach turn into moths as I recall the other conversation I had with Lexi. I wouldn't be surprised if she gave Aiden a heads up about it. I'm dreading leaving this spot and consider pretending to be asleep until I leave for work.

No, Charlie. You need to break up with Aiden. There will never be a good time to end things.

I stand while I still have the courage and walk out to find him sitting at the kitchen counter. He's not eating or looking at his phone, just staring blankly into the distance.

"Hey." I try to get his attention. "Can we talk?" I cut to the chase, afraid if I waste time with pleasantries, I'll chicken out at the last moment.

He breaks his trance and looks at me with a curious expression. Maybe Lexi didn't give him a heads up after all.

"Sure, what's up? Everything okay?" he asks, concern in his voice. He must sense something is off.

"Yeah. Well, no, actually," I correct myself. "Could we go sit on the couch?" I walk over to the living room, and he follows silently, as if the comfort of our couch will help ease the pain of what I'm about to say.

"Aiden, I really don't know how to say this to you, so I'm just going to get straight to it." My eyes fall to the floor; I don't have the heart to look at his face. "I've been unhappy for a while now, and I know you've been feeling the same way," I pause. He cocks his head in confusion. "I think the situation last week only validated my feelings and put things into perspective for me."

He opens his mouth to say something, but I cut him off. "Please, Aiden. Don't say anything until I'm done. I really need to get this off my chest." My eyes start to well with tears. "I really don't think we should get married. I don't think we're right for each other anymore. I feel like we've been going through the motions for too long, and it's time to be honest with ourselves." I choke on my words, hot streams of tears running down my face.

I peek up to see a horrified look on Aiden's face. "Wha-what are you talking about, Charlie?" His voice cracks. "If you're unhappy, fine, but don't tell me I've been unhappy! You just wake up and spring this shit on me? How the hell can you do this?" He jumps from his seat and backs away, face bright red, as if he's been hanging upside down on monkey bars.

"Don't just come up to me and fucking shit on our entire relationship! I love you and love our life!" he shouts, the sting of betrayal painted on his face. "Why the hell would you want to throw all that away?"

"What life?" I interject. "We hardly talk or see each other, and when we do, we're just on our phones! How is that a relationship? You never seem happy to see me, do nice things for me, or even think about me! You may say you love me, but your actions say otherwise!" I shout back, face soaked with salty tears. "The whole reason that crash happened is because I was too tired of fighting with you! I knew if I pushed calling a car, you would just shut me down, because *Aiden* always knows best. Well, I've had it." I try to calm myself so our neighbors don't hear us screaming and call the police. I can see the hurt in his eyes. His gaze fell to the floor as soon as I mentioned the car accident.

"You think I don't feel horrible about what I did?" he mutters. "You think I don't regret the moment I got behind that wheel?" His tone turns sour. "I would give everything to take it back, Charlie! Is that what you wanted to hear?"

"No! What I wanted is for you not to have done it in the first place, to not take all my suggestions as personal attacks on you. Don't ignore me. I want you to *want* to be with me," I say. "I'm sorry, Aiden, but there's no way that we can stay together." I pull my old tee shirt up to dry my wet face.

"Do you really think I'm the problem? Maybe I'd be more interested in spending time together if you weren't such a bitch all the time. All you ever do is remind me I'm not good enough! You make sure to point out every one of my mistakes and rub it in my face. You never appreciate me for who I am or what I have to offer." A vein appears on his forehead, which usually only shows up when he's truly angry.

He turns around and punches a hole in the drywall. "How dare you! We could have worked on this together. That's what marriage is all about: working through the problems, not just giving up on each other. You should have said something sooner. Now what am I supposed to tell my family, huh? You just don't care?"

"Aiden. I'm so sorry, but it would be wrong of me to marry you knowing how I feel. You deserve to marry someone who is crazy about you," I say. "And I deserve the same. You'll always hold a special place in my heart, but right now, I need to do what's best for me." I bring my hands to my chest, as if to offer myself support. "Are you oka—" I step closer to see his face.

"Just go," he cuts me off. "Please leave. I don't want to see you right now. Please go away." He continues crying into the wall.

"Okay," I say quietly, backing into the bedroom, gently closing the door behind me before falling onto my bed to cry. I bawl into my pillow uncontrollably—not because I made a mistake, but because I'm letting go of such an important part of my life, and it hurts. I hate that I hurt him like this. I wasn't prepared to see such pain on his face. It left me feeling more anxious and guilty than before.

To make matters worse, I still have to go to work.

25

CHARLIE
THURSDAY, JUNE 22ND: 6:45 P.M.

I'M STANDING OUTSIDE of Henry's hospital room, hesitant to go in. My eyes are still puffy from crying myself to sleep, and I'm worried he'll say something about it. Maybe I can keep my head down to avoid eye contact. I can be in and out before he even has a chance to ask me what's wrong.

I take a deep breath and try my best not to overthink. I smile as I open his room door. His bed is covered in papers, like he's been grading homework assignments. "As promised, I brought you a carne asada burrito and some tacos from the Mexican spot down the street," I say, trying my best to avoid his gaze.

His face is buried in papers, hair disheveled, as if he's been working from his bed all day. "Oh hey." He smiles without looking up. "You're a god send." He exhales as he drops the papers on his lap, finally admitting defeat. His smile quickly fades when he notices my swollen face.

"Hey, are you okay?" His tone softens. "Charlie?"

I briefly imagine diving into his strong arms and crying into his chest. I could really use a hug right now.

I take a moment before responding, afraid I'll burst into tears the moment I open my mouth. "I-" I choke. I can feel all the tension building in my throat, waiting to be released. "I-" I stutter again before forcing a smile. "I'm fine."

"You don't look fine. It looks like you've been crying," he persists.

Okay, what am I waiting for? This is what I wanted, right? I need to just come out and say it. "Aiden and I broke up."

His eyes widen as he processes what I just said. "Oh..." His voice trails off. He runs his fingers through his dark waves as he contemplates his response. "Um, I'm sorry. Are you okay?" His brown eyes narrow as he tries to read my movements.

"Yes," I respond quickly, trying to reassure him. "I mean, I'm not sad about the breakup. It was my decision. I guess I'm just feeling overwhelmed by all the sudden changes." I set the bag of fast food on his bedside table and walk to the computer to check his chart. "I've been wanting to leave him for a long time," I clarify, "but it's actually real now. I'm not sure what's next." I look everywhere but his eyes.

His breathing grows heavy, and the space between us suddenly feels smaller. I peek up to see him staring intently at the wall in front of him, heat radiating from his body.

"Sorry to unload on you like that." I grab the blood pressure cuff to check his levels. "So, anyway. I'm just going to check your blood pressure real quick." I sniffle. "Any pain today?" I try to change the subject to spare myself the additional embarrassment.

"Charlie," Henry says as I wrap the cuff around his firm bicep.

"Yeah?" I answer reluctantly, unsure of what to expect.

"I'm sorry you're in pain right now, and this may be too soon, but I'm glad he's gone," he says sternly. "I know this is probably the last thing on your mind right now, but when you're ready—and there is no rush—I want to take you out."

I wasn't sure how he would react to my news, but I wasn't

expecting him to ask me out while I cry about my breakup. "Hm..." I think out loud. "That's sweet of you." I take a step back. Unsure how to respond, I panic and switch back into nurse mode. "Um, I should get going. I need to finish making my rounds. I'll be back to check on you soon." I smile professionally and leave.

How am I supposed to respond to that?

———

I feel like I'm operating on auto-pilot. I know I'm working and doing the things I'm supposed to do, but I wouldn't be able to recall any conversations I've had with patients today. My body is simply relying on muscle memory at this point.

Sheila will probably get suspicious when she can't find me in the break room, but I don't care. I don't want to talk to her about the situation with Aiden. If I do, I know she'll ask about Henry, and I'm not ready for that conversation either. Not yet, anyway.

I look at my watch and am relieved to see it's almost time for my break. I've been running around my floor all night because we're understaffed. We had one nurse call out sick while another is gone on PTO. I'm dying to sit down and rest my aching feet. All the crying earlier also made me drowsy and desperate for sleep.

I mindlessly walk around my section, conducting checkups before my break. My watch vibrates, letting me know it's finally time to clock out. I let out a sigh of relief and jog to the break-room to grab myself a cup of coffee to go. I'd like to grab it before Sheila sees me and tries to stop me for chit chat.

I toss the coffee pod into the machine and watch eagerly as it slowly churns out the hot black liquid. The sound of laughter grows louder as they get closer to the break room, and I freeze, but they stop right outside of the door to finish their conversation.

"Phew." I grab my Styrofoam cup as soon as it's filled and speedwalk out the other door, not even bothering to empty the machine.

I don't want to speak to anyone but Henry right now. I have no idea what I'm going to say to him, but maybe an apology for rushing out earlier is a good place to start.

The hallway seems unusually quiet as I make my way to his room. The only sounds are coming from the nurses' station, where the two mean girls on shift are whispering to each other. I'm about to reach for Henry's door when one of them calls out to me. "I thought you went on break?"

I look to see both women staring wide-eyed as they wait for an explanation.

"Oh, yeah… I, uh, think I forgot something. I'm just going to check real quick, and then I'll be out of here," I say as I back into his room.

Snickers come from their area, but I choose to ignore them. The nurses here gossip as much as my mother's book club.

Henry is sitting up in his bed, one light shining down on him as he reads a textbook. It looks like he's about to break into song with the spotlight on him like that.

"Hey," I say as I quietly close the door behind me. "I wasn't sure if you'd be awake." I slowly approach his bed like a child who had a bad dream.

"Nah, I'm not really tired." He rubs the back of his neck.

"Yeah, I can see that. What are you reading?" I try to get a look at the cover.

"Oh, this?" His eyes light up. "It's a book about teaching outside the box. I try to stay up-to-date on the best practices and am always looking for new ideas. It's hard to hold kids' attention, ya know? It's important to get creative." He smiles as he shows me the book.

It's cute to see how passionate he is about his job. It must be a great feeling to do something you're so passionate about.

"You really love teaching, huh? What got you into it?" I ask as I sit in the chair next to him.

"My mother, actually. She was a creative writing professor at NYU and inspired my love for literature. I used to sit in on her lectures as a kid, listen to her teach. Instead of traditional bedtime stories, she would often read her students' papers to me. It's a fun memory to look back on." His eyes glisten, as if he wants to cry.

"Wow, that's really beautiful. Your mom sounds like a great woman." I smile.

"Yeah, she is," he reminisces. "So, how are you? Are you feeling better than earlier?" His thick eyebrow raises slightly.

"Yeah, I just..." I pause, trying to think about where this sentence is going.

"Are you okay?" He sits up to get a better look at me.

"Yeah." I quickly wave off his concern. "I want to apologize for how I left earlier. I was just taken by surprise and didn't know how to react."

"No, please, don't apologize. You must think I'm a douchebag for coming on to you when you were literally crying," he says sheepishly. "I'm actually pretty embarrassed, so maybe we can just pretend it never happened?"

"Don't get me wrong," I say, "going out with you sounds nice, but..."

"No, I understand," he says. "How are you feeling now?"

"Um, better than earlier." I can feel my eyes welling up again, but I look away, so hopefully, he won't notice. "I told Aiden I don't want to marry him."

"And was that the right thing to do?" Henry asks in a kind voice, one I imagine he would use to console one of his students.

"Yes. Neither of us were happy." A tear escapes my eye, but I quickly catch it with my sleeve. "We just don't work together anymore. I was tired of being sad and knew I had to back out before it was too late." I try my best to smile. I'm shocked I'm sharing so much information with someone I barely know.

I can feel Henry's eyes tracking my body movements, analyzing me.

"I'm sorry, Charlie. That must be rough." He continues staring in my direction, as if hoping our eyes meet, but they don't. I won't let them. I'm terrified to look back and get trapped in his honey gaze again. His eyes are beautiful, but staring into someone's soul like that makes me uncomfortable. I don't like imagining what they see in me.

"Erm, can I ask you something?" he says sheepishly.

"Yeah, of course," I answer back.

"Is there another reason you left him?"

This time, I don't avoid his eyes. I pinch my lips together as I try to gather my thoughts. I'm so nervous; I don't want to screw up and say something stupid.

"Well, if I'm being honest, you are a partial reason. This may sound silly, but..." I hesitate. "Meeting you made me realize how unhappy I was with Aiden and how long I've felt that way. I know that sounds stupid, since we barely know each other." I exhale. "This isn't me asking you out or anything. I needed to get out of that relationship regardless," I clarify. I don't want to scare him off by acting like I broke off my engagement for him after only knowing each other for a week. I'm scaring myself enough already.

I look at him, trying to get a read on his face. He looks around the room and runs his fingers through his scruff. "Hmm..." He looks out the window. "So, just to be clear...you wouldn't want to go out with me?" he teases. "I mean, come on. I'm not totally damaged goods." He laughs as he points to his bandaged leg hanging in a sling. His laughter is contagious, and soon enough, I'm cracking up too.

I don't know why I'm laughing so hard. Maybe my brain snapped after all the crying earlier, who knows. We're obviously being loud, because the woman from earlier walks in.

"Is everything alright?" she asks frantically. We both fall silent and look at her in surprise, like two children caught playing past their bedtime.

"Did you find what you were looking for?" she asks with a fake smile and a raised eyebrow.

"Erm, still looking," I joke.

She scoffs and turns away to walk out of the room, closing the door behind her.

"Did I get you in trouble?" Henry asks.

"No." I try to catch my breath. "Don't worry about it. I'm on my break." I wave off his concerns. "But I should be getting back soon anyway. My break's over in ten minutes. Thanks for letting me visit and dump all my trauma onto you." I catch myself picking my lip again and immediately drop my hands.

He laughs. "Anytime. Really." His dark eyes are warm and comforting, like a cup of hot cocoa.

I stand up from my seat to leave, but he interrupts. "Hey, Charlie?"

"Yeah?" I turn around a little too eagerly.

"I was serious earlier. I'm sorry about you and your ex, but to tell you the truth, I'm kind of relieved. I know that sounds selfish, and there's no rush whatsoever, but when you're feeling up for it, I would love to take you to dinner. Ya know, after I can move around again." He chuckles. "Which should be soon, since my knee gets fixed first thing tomorrow."

"Thanks, Henry. I would love that. I'll stop by tomorrow

before my shift to see how you're doing. Good night." Heat radiates from my chest and flows into my face. I don't want the other nurses to see my flushed cheeks, so I quietly open the door and swiftly glide out toward the breakroom, pretending not to notice the two women exchanging judgmental glances.

I walk past the breakroom, where Sheila sits at a table, sipping on her coffee.

"Hey, where'd you sneak off to?" she asks suspiciously.

"Oh, hey. Just thought I'd eat in my car today." I flash a quick smile and keep walking to evade any more questions. I'm feeling too good and don't want to give anyone the chance to ruin that. It's not like Sheila would try to make me feel bad about anything, but I suppose I'm feeling guilty over my feelings for Henry.

But why? Why am I feeling guilty? Aiden's the one who kissed another woman. At least I had the decency to end things before even thinking about starting something with someone. Plus, Henry and I haven't even kissed; we've just been getting to know each other. I try to convince myself I'm doing nothing wrong, but I'm having trouble buying it.

I roll up my sleeves and get back to work. Maybe I'll stop thinking about it if I keep myself busy.

AIDEN

FRIDAY, JUNE 22ND: 1:25 A.M.

I watch the ceiling fan spin out of control above me as I lay motionless in bed. I don't know how I'm going to wake up for work in the morning when I can't fall asleep.

How can I? My mind keeps replaying what Charlie said. She wants to leave? Just like that? I feel so helpless, like I'm dealing with a complete stranger who doesn't care about me at all. So many bad thoughts are consuming my mind. I don't know how I'm going to deal with all the embarrassment.

I grab my phone to text Lexi.

Hey, you up?

She's younger than me, so I'm sure she's still up. I, on the other hand, am usually in bed by nine, because I'm useless without a full eight hours of sleep.

Hey, yeah, I am. What's up?

Her message pops up almost immediately. I can always count on Lexi to make me feel better.

I ended things with Charlie and just need someone to talk to.

Oh, I'm sorry.

I was expecting a bigger reaction from her. I really don't want to be home alone. I'm driving myself crazy laying in this bed. All I'm going to do is think about her and her betrayal.

Are you doing anything right now?

Not really. Wanna come over? I can make you some coffee or tea, and we can talk about it.

She offers.
I let out a sigh of relief.

Yeah, I would love that. Thanks.

I jump off the bed, grab my coat, and run out the door.

"So can I grab you a drink or anything?" Lexi asks from her kitchen as I toss my things on her couch.

"Uh, just some water would be good. Thanks."

She walks out of the kitchen wearing red silk pajama shorts and a matching crop top, two cups in hand. "Here you go." She hands me a glass and signals for me to sit on the couch.

"So what happened?" She sits on the cushion furthest from me, waiting for an answer.

"Well, to be honest, I just couldn't stop thinking about the other night." Her mouth drops. "When you kissed me, it made me realize how unhappy I've been with Charlie. I guess I've been feeling this way for a while and thought I should be honest with her before it was too late and we got married."

"What did Charlie think about the kiss?" Her eyes squint, as if she knows something I don't.

Why would she ask that? "Um, I don't know and I don't care." I brush it off.

She scoots closer and lays her hand on mine, caressing my fingers with her thumb. "Did you two talk about it?" Her blue eyes widen.

"Um, no. Why would I tell her? I already decided to leave her; I didn't want to hurt her more," I say nervously. What's with the third degree?

"Interesting." She smiles smugly.

I try my best to fake a smile and lean in a little closer.

She bites her lip. "I didn't say anything to you about this because I figured she would, but she knows about our kiss," she says nonchalantly. "She texted me the next morning and asked me point blank." She shrugs like it's no big deal.

"What?" I ask, unsure if I heard her correctly. "And what did you tell her?" I'm suddenly breathless.

"The truth. I didn't want to lie to her." She scoots closer to me and moves her hand to my leg in a poor attempt at comfort. "But it's okay now. You said it yourself. You weren't happy with her. Now, you and I can see if there's anything here." Her eyes glisten with hope.

I look away to hide my sudden rage. I can't believe Lexi got involved. This is all her fault.

"Are you okay?" she asks in a soft voice. "I thought you would be happy about this." The corners of her lips fall in disappointment.

Is this the real reason Charlie broke it off? *No.* If this was the reason, then she would have said so instead of all that other bullshit about us being unhappy. This is what she wanted, regardless of the kiss. Charlie said so herself: she doesn't want to be with me. Why should I want to be with her when I have a gorgeous bombshell who wants me the way I am?

My anger is back on Charlie again.

"I'm sorry, Lexi. I am happy." I place my hand over hers. "Of course I want to be with you."

She lunges toward me and plants a wet kiss on my lips before I can say anything else. I guess this is good, because I have no idea what I was going to say next.

I follow her lead and run my fingers through her silky blonde hair, pulling her face closer to mine. She swings her long leg over my hip and sits on my lap. The heat from her thighs radiates into my lower half.

I grab a hand full of her hair and pull her head back to kiss her neck, slowly making my way to her collar bone. She lets out a soft groan as she slides off her shirt and tosses it across the room.

I don't know why, but all I can think about is Charlie and what she's doing right now. Would she care if she saw me with Lexi? Would she be jealous and regret her decision? I decide to pull myself out of my head and re-focus on the half-naked woman in front of me.

27

CHARLIE

FRIDAY, JUNE 22ND: 7:25 A.M.

I'm exhausted and covered in dried vomit. Today was not an easy one. I drop my clothes in the washer and hop in the steaming hot shower to scrub the day away. I didn't see Aiden's car in the driveway when I got here, so I'm guessing he left for work early to avoid seeing me.

My body feels weak and heavy. I sit at the bottom of the shower, hugging my knees as the hot water pours over my head. I wish I could go to sleep in this steamy cocoon of my own making.

Henry pops into my mind as I watch the water race down my arms. I've really loved getting to know him, but that night still lingers in the back of my mind. Am I really going to keep this secret for the rest of my life? What happens if the police catches us? I would go to prison, and Henry would never trust me or any woman again. My life is so confusing right now, and I have no idea what to do. The only other person who can understand what I'm going through doesn't want to talk to me.

Don't cry, Charlie. You chose not to tell the police the truth and to leave Aiden. You did this to yourself and need to deal with the consequences. If—no, *when*—Henry finds out, you'll have no one to blame but yourself.

I drag myself out of the shower and wrap my hair in a towel. I'm too tired to blow-dry it, so it looks like I'm going to bed with a damp head. I belly flop onto my comforter and grab my phone. Henry goes into surgery soon, so I should wish him luck.

> Hey, I know you're going into surgery and just wanted to tell you you're in good hands. I'll see you tonight.

I hit send and then bury my face in my fluffy pillow.

28

HENRY

FRIDAY, JUNE 22ND: 9:05 A.M.

"Good morning, sunshine. Are you ready to get that knee fixed?" a nurse jokes as she walks into the room. "How are you feeling?"

"I'm feeling fine. Just ready to get this over with," I groan.

I wish I could have gotten this taken care of sooner, but the doctors wanted to wait until my concussion symptoms subsided before putting me under general anesthesia. My palms sweat as I think about it. I want to trust the doctors, but it's hard to after they failed my mother so many times. I check my phone before the nurses take me to the OR and see a message from Charlie.

> Hey, I know you're going into surgery, and I just wanted to tell you you're in good hands. I'll check in on you during my shift tonight.

I can't help but smile.

The nurses wheel me into a cold room and help lift me onto a narrow and unwelcoming bed just wide enough to hold my body, with two armrests that strap my hands into place. It makes me feel uneasy, like I'm about to be tortured for information I don't have.

"Alright, I'm going to place a mask over your face, okay? It may feel a little hard to breathe at first, but try to relax," a pale man with gray stubble and a blank stare says as he towers over my head. "Take a deep breath and count backwards from ten," he says as he tightly presses the mask against my face.

"Okay," I respond, trying to ignore the urge to gasp for more air. "Ten. Nine. Eight. Seven. Six. Fi..." My vision gets blurry and my head begins to feel fuzzy.

I wonder what Charlie's doing?

———

I open my eyes and see a cloudy figure leaning over me. The lights behind their head are almost blinding, so I close my eyes to ease the strain.

My vision is much clearer when I open them again. Wait a second; I think I'm in a different room. Did I pass out? My brain feels foggy, and I have no sense of time. I look around the room to see the sun is still in full force. It must be around mid-afternoon, which means I lost most of the day.

A familiar face walks into the room with a cup of coffee. "You're awake! Thank goodness." My sister rushes over and gives me a tight hug.

"Uh, careful. Surgery, remember?" I groan as she squeezes me in her arms.

"I'm so sorry I couldn't come sooner." She drags a chair next to my bedside.

"It's okay. You're here now, and that's all that matters. Thanks for coming, sis." I reach out my hand to hold hers. I can feel a tear escape and don't try to hide it. It's been a rough year, and I'm really glad she's here. She lives in the U.K., and I don't get to see her often, since she's so busy working at the U.S. Embassy in London.

"How ya feeling, kid?" she asks, combing my damp hair back with her fingers. She was like a second mother to me, took care of me when our mom was busy writing or on book tours. It feels nice to finally see a familiar face around here.

"I'm okay." My voice cracks. "I mean, it could have been a lot worse. A knee is worth sacrificing over my life." I laugh, but I can see sadness on her face as I say that.

"Yeah, you're right. I'm just glad you're okay. I took some time off work so I can stick around and take care of you." She squeezes my hand.

"Thank you, but you don't have to do that. I'll be okay," I try to convince her, though I secretly would love to have her stay for a while. Who knows when I'll see her again?

"No, no. I'll stay. Plus, I haven't seen your place since you moved, so it'll be nice to see what you've been up to! How are you liking it here? It's so different from New York. Are you seeing anyone?" She perks up as she tries to get the latest scoop of drama in my life. How typical of her. I can't help but laugh at the excitement on her face.

"Um, well, actually, it's a funny story." I rub my arm nervously. "After my accident, a woman found me on the road and called 9-1-1. Well, it turns out, she's actually a nurse at this hospital. We've been talking ever since." I feel like a giddy school boy talking about a crush. I try to hide my blush by casually glancing out the window.

"Woah, are you serious? So I guess there is a silver lining in this situation." She leans back in her chair and crosses her arms in disbelief.

"Yeah, I guess so. She works the night shift, so she's going to visit me during her break tonight."

"Ooh, okay. Well, I'm glad to hear you haven't been totally alone here." She smiles mischievously.

"How are things with Dave and the kids?" I change the subject.

She rolls her eyes. "Oh, Dave is Dave, and the kids are as crazy as ever! He's being a trooper, though, handling them on his own for this long."

Her kids are pretty wild, like her. Avery was mature in the sense that she took care of me a lot of the time, but she also has a crazy personality and a lot of energy. It makes sense that her kids have the same head-strong mindset.

A firm knock hits the door. "Yeah? Come in," I announce.

A short, slender man in a gray blazer and pink tie enters the room, followed by a taller middle-aged man in a custom-tailored navy suit. The small man's entrance is overshadowed by his hulking accomplice trailing in after. "Can I help you?" I ask.

"Hi," the shorter one says. "We spoke on the phone a couple of days ago. I'm Muriel Smith, and this is Mr. Whitman." I definitely thought he was a woman when we spoke on the phone the other day.

"Um, yeah, I remember, but why are you here? I never gave you an answer about the interview," I say, irritated by their brazen disregard for my privacy. Now I definitely don't want to talk to them. *Pricks.*

My sister looks at them and then looks back to me in confusion. "Who are they?" she whispers from the side of her mouth.

"Yes, about that—" Muriel starts, but my sister jumps up and cuts him off.

"Thank you guys for coming by." She walks over to them with arms open, as if to herd them out like a group of children. "Can you both give us a moment? I was in the middle of a discussion with my brother. Please wait in the hall, and I'll grab you in a second." She leads them out the door.

"But—" the short one tries to interject.

"Thank you," she says in her best customer service voice as

she closes the door in their faces. She really went full mom mode there.

She lets out a long sigh and rejoins me at my bedside. "Okay, so you wanna explain what's going on?" She raises her eyebrows, as if waiting for me to confess something.

"Um, well, the big guy is some local politician who wanted to talk with me about my accident. They said they wanted to bring more attention to my situation and pressure the police to prioritize my case. They think if they appeal to the public, maybe someone will come forward with information," I explain.

"Well, that's amazing! Why didn't you call them back? If someone with a following is willing to help you, you should take it. We need all the support we can get to find the person who left you for dead." Her nostrils are flaring, so I don't think she'll be willing to hear me out on this.

"Yeah, but—"

"No buts!" she cuts me off. "Henry, someone hit you with their car and left you to die in the middle of the street. We need to find the sick fuck who did this to you." Tears well up in her eyes. "It's not fair. If this increases the chances they get caught by even 1%, it's worth it." She wraps my hand in both her palms. "Please. Please, talk to them." Her eyes are so sad, I can't possibly say no. Maybe she's right. What's the harm in having a conversation?

"Okay." I sigh in defeat. "Go ahead and get them."

"Okay, great. Thank you." She smiles and kisses me on the cheek before letting them back in.

"Gentlemen. He's ready to speak with you." She holds open the door as they enter the room. The larger man in the back radiates confidence, reminding me of a superhero.

"Hey there," he says in a low but stern voice. "My name is John Whitman, and I just want to start by saying I'm so sorry for showing up unannounced like this, but I think this injustice is too great to ignore." His speech sounds well-rehearsed, as if there was a news camera on him right now. "If it's okay with you, I would love to have a conversation about your accident and share your story with my supporters." He stands at the edge of my bed, waiting for a reply. His blue eyes and thick gold brows are intense.

"Uh, yeah, sure." I give my sister the side eye. "Why not." I rub my hands on my thighs to dry my clammy palms.

"Great! I really think this is a good decision." He points to the small man before him.

"Uh, right. Henry, is it okay if I record this conversation?" he says through his nose as he pulls out a collapsible ring light from his leather satchel.

Why do I feel like a kid being interviewed by teachers who are trying to find out if everything's okay at home?

"Yeah, that's fine," I assure him.

I still feel pretty groggy from the surgery and don't have the mind to get into detail. I wonder if they chose this time visit intentionally, hoping I would be too loopy from the drugs to resist. The thought leaves a sour taste in my mouth.

29

CHARLIE

SATURDAY, JUNE 23RD: 12:45 A.M.

THE WHITE **KRDC** News van catches my eye as I pull into the hospital parking lot, and I almost consider turning around and calling out sick. It's like they're following me, making sure I don't forget what I've done.

Every surface of my body is covered in sweat as I discretely walk past the reporter from before, Patricia Hernandez, hoping she doesn't recognize me. I hear her mention a familiar name as I walk into the lobby. *John Whitman.* That's the guy who's running for mayor...and who asked to talk with Henry. Is he the reason for the news van?

Questions swirl in my mind as I make my way to the locker room.

"What's with the news crew?" I ask Amanda as I toss my bag into my locker.

Amanda peers at me as she slicks her blonde hair into a high ponytail. "John Whitman had a press conference outside earlier, talking about that hurt jogger of yours and looking after teachers and stuff."

"Oh, yeah?" I try to act casual. "That's weird. Did he say anything else?"

"Eh, I was too distracted by his gorgeous face to actually listen." She shrugs with a smile and leaves the room.

Henry and the news crew occupy my mind as I start an IV on a patient. While it's not national news, it sure feels that way when every TV in the hospital is airing it. With a small town like Redwell, stories like this have a way of running for longer than they should. One time, someone drunkenly crashed into the town's "Welcome to Redwell" sign, and that was the talked about for a month. There were even rallies and fundraisers help to fix it.

"Ow!" the elderly woman in bed shrieks. "Will you watch where you poke that thing?"

"I'm so sorry. I'm having a little trouble finding your vein," I lie, because I got lost in thought and forgot to pay attention to what I was doing. *Get it together, Charlie, and stop screwing around before you get yourself in trouble.* I take a deep calming breath to re-center myself, trying my best to ignore her grimace.

"Okay, that'll do it. I'll come back in a little while to check on you." I smile while I cautiously back away, as if her frail body may leap at me the moment I turn my back.

"Please don't." The woman sarcastically smiles back as she waves me off.

I'm not offended by her comment. I get it. She has an actual reason to dislike me, unlike the other 98% of grumpy patients I get. I guess that's just something that comes with the territory. You can't expect all sick people to be happy about getting poked and prodded. I bite my tongue and gracefully walk out of the room to show her words don't phase me.

"Hey, you taking your break soon?" Sheila looks at me with wide eyes, as if expecting a gift.

"Yeah, but I have some things to take care of, so I won't be eating here." I try to keep it short and walk to my next patient's room to avoid any more small talk.

She smiles and speedwalks to catch up. "Some things to take care of or *someone*?" She emphasizes the word with an excited look in her eyes.

I stop in my tracks and look at her. Those damn women must have blabbed! "Um, what are you talking about?" I try to play dumb to see how much she knows.

"Oh, don't be coy. I know you went to visit that sexy little thing off the clock. So, is there something you want to tell me?" Her eyebrows raise higher than they're meant to go.

I look around us and pull her to the side and out of the walkway. "Okay, look. I promise I was going to tell you, but Aiden and I broke up, and I've kind of been talking to Henry about it. He's been a really good friend," I try to explain myself.

"What?" she yells. "You bro—"

I slap my hand over her mouth to stop her from finishing her sentence.

"Sheila. Please keep this to yourself for now. As you obviously know, there is no such thing as privacy around here, so I would like to figure this out without the whole hospital gossiping about it. Okay?" I look at her dead in the eye. "Please promise me. If you agree to do this, I will tell you everything you want to know later."

She still looks puzzled. "Okay." She smiles as she holds up her pinky for me to promise.

"Thank you!" I shout as I walk toward my next patient's room.

"But you better call me on your way home so you can explain yourself!" She points to me as she walks back to her section.

"I promise!" I almost fall over in relief. I'm sure there are already plenty of rumors going around, but I don't care.

I look at my watch, happy to see my break is approaching. I walk into the next room and try my best to focus.

"Good morning," I whisper as I walk into the patient's dark room. "Sorry to wake you. How are you feeling, Mr. Wilson?" I go to his bedside to get a better look at the nape of his neck. "I'm here to check on your incision. I'm just going to move your head for a moment, okay? Let me know if there's any discomfort."

"No worries, darling," he says groggily. "It makes no difference to me." His round belly bounces as he lets out a phlegmy cough. "Ow, ow," he winces.

"I'm sorry. Sudden bursts like that may hurt for a while. I'll give you a little more medicine for the pain," I say. "Okay, I'll come back later to check on you." My watch starts vibrating as soon as I leave his room, as if it waited to avoid interrupting me.

I speedwalk to the locker room to touch up my hair and face. I'm eager to visit Henry and see how he's feeling after the surgery.

I don't see any nurses in the hall, so I leap to his cracked door and slide in, taking a second to catch my breath. "Henry?" I say cautiously.

He looks up from the stack of papers on his lap. "Oh, hey." He smiles and sets his papers to the side.

"How are you feeling? Are you back to grading papers already?" I step in.

"Oh, these? No. These are letters from my students. The sub had them all write me letters to fill me in on what I've missed. They're really sweet." He smiles as he looks at the colorful pile.

"Wow, your students must really care about you. Hopefully, you can go back to teaching soon." I inch closer. "So, how's your knee?"

His leg is elevated, covered in the scratchy, thin white hospital sheet.

"The doctor said it went well, and I'm not feeling any pain right now, thanks to the meds," he says as he draws the covers back to expose his tatted legs, which are stronger and more defined than they looked in that Instagram photo. It also looks like he's gotten a few more tattoos since. "I don't think it looks too bad." He smiles like a kid showing off his battle scars.

I scoot in to get a closer look. The inner side of his right knee is swollen and purple, with twelve dissolvable stitches. Above that, on his thigh, is tattoo of a black skull laying in the sand, surrounded by the words 'Dead men don't bite.' That's the tattoo I saw in his hiking photo but couldn't make out. He also has a large moth on his left thigh, as well as some small abstract ones placed randomly around his leg.

"What does this mean?" I point to the skull.

"Oh, it's a quote from the book *Treasure Island*. It was the story that got me into reading."

"Hmm, I see." I gently place my index finger on the top of the skull. "Does this hurt?" My finger is nowhere near his incision, but I ask anyway.

His eyes look surprised I'm touching him. To be honest, I'm surprised too.

"Uh, no. That doesn't hurt," he says.

I don't respond and instead start tracing the outline with my fingertip. "It's a beautiful tattoo. I love the art style," I say, not looking away from the image. His skin breaks into goosebumps beneath my fingertip as I gently move it across his thigh.

"Thanks," he says. His brown eyes narrow as they focus on my hand, trying to figure out what I'll do next.

"What do the others mean?" I ask.

"Um, the moth is an inside joke. My mom always hated

moths, so my dad said he would come back as one when he died just to mess with her," he says, still distracted by my touch. "I got it after he passed a few years ago."

That story is both tragic and sweet. His parents sound like they were good together. I'd like to find that someday.

"The artwork is beautiful. Do all your tattoos have a story like that?" I ask as I examine the other markings, as if I'm carefully inspecting various paintings in a museum.

"No. The others are just because I liked them," he says.

Before I can get a better look, he sits forward and wraps his large hands around mine. His fingers are rough and calloused. He gently pulls my hands closer to his chest, guiding me to his bedside, our faces now inches apart.

"H-Herny?" I stutter in confusion.

"I've wanted to kiss you since the moment I first saw you, but I couldn't. I didn't want to screw anything up for you," he whispers.

The hairs on the back of my neck stand, and my nipples peak through my scrubs. I can feel his heartbeat intensify under the palm of my hand. I've wanted to kiss him badly too. I lean forward and press my lips against his, sliding my hands up to cup his stubbled cheeks. His skin radiates heat and smells like coffee.

He wraps his left arm around my waist and pulls me closer to his side. My hip bone is now crushed against the bed rail, but I don't care. I'm both surprised and turned on by his raw strength. His delicious lips move with mine as if we've done this a thousand times before.

He runs one hand through my hair while the other strokes my lower back. I reluctantly pull away. "I'm sorry. We shouldn't be doing this here. I could get in serious trouble." I try to stop myself before going back in for more.

He flips my hair behind my back and shoves his face into my neck, lightly biting just above my collar bone. I clutch his chest and let out a soft giggle. My hand gently grazes his body, sliding down from his chest. I want to feel every muscle on his body. I can feel him getting hard at my touch.

"God, you smell amazing," he says, face still buried in my neck. I can feel his hot breath on my ear and nearly faint.

"Thanks," I say before pulling his head back and going back in for a kiss. His lips taste like black coffee, and I can't get enough. I have to stop myself from climbing into his hospital bed.

A knock at his door interrupts us, and I immediately jump away from him, bumping the metal chair as I step back. A nurse pulls back the curtains to see us both out of breath and Henry obviously trying to cover his groin with the papers on his lap to hide his excitement.

She looks at me, then him, then back at me with a slightly raised brow. "Let's not forget how we conduct ourselves here," she says to me, completely ignoring Henry.

"It's not what you think..." I stumble.

"I'm going to give you a moment, sir, but I'll be back to check your knee. Visiting hours are over." She rolls her eyes before turning away, leaving both the curtains and door wide open on her way out.

"I'm sorry. I shouldn't have done that, especially not here." He sighs. "I don't know what came over me," he says, eyes riddled with regret.

"Don't worry about it." I comb my hair back with my fingers, still out of breath. "Nurses have done a lot worse here." I try to play it off. "We'll continue this when you're out of here."

"I like the sound of that." He smiles.

"Well, I should probably head out. I'm glad the surgery went well." I turn away and head for the door.

"Have a good rest of your shift," he says.

I walk out and smile at the nurses giving me the stink eye from their desk. "It's not what you think." I roll my eyes as I walk back to the elevator, failing to hide the mischievous grin growing on my face.

30

CHARLIE

SATURDAY, JUNE 23RD: 7:15 A.M.

BUTTERFLIES SWIRL in my stomach on the drive home as I replay that scene in my head. I can't believe he grabbed me like that. His hands were so firm yet gentle. A shiver jolts through my body as I remember the feel of his touch.

My phone vibrates, disrupting my thoughts. I ignore it and decide to check when I get home, but it starts vibrating uncontrollably. I take a peek at the screen to see Sheila's name. Fuck, I forgot to call her.

"Hello?" I answer through my car's Bluetooth.

"Hey, you done with work?" she asks. "I got too impatient waiting for you to call. Tell me what's going on with you and Aiden." She sounds confused.

"Well, I thought about what you told me in the break room, and you were right. I'm not happy with Aiden, and I haven't been for a while. So we broke up like a couple of days ago."

The other end of the line is silent. "Are you feeling okay?" she asks calmly.

"Yeah, I think so. I mean, it's still confusing for me, but I know I made the right decision. Plus, he kissed someone else, so I think it's safe to assume he's ready for this too." I don't know why I'm trying to defend my actions as if I did something wrong. It's not like Sheila is going to judge me.

"Wait, really? I can't believe I missed so much!" Her voice perks up. "Okay, so many questions, but first, when did this happen and who did he kiss?"

"It was with some coworker after an office event, but it may have gone further than that. I honestly don't know what to believe," I say as I pull into my driveway. I transfer the call to my cell and walk into the house, tossing my stuff on the floor next to the kitchen counter before I belly flop onto the couch, waiting for her to respond.

"Wow, I'm sorry, Charlie. I know you said you're ready to break up and everything, but that must have still hurt you on some level." Her voice softens.

"Actually, no. I wasn't sad at all, and I think that's what made me realize it was time to break up. I gave him back his ring and everything." I sigh and dig my face into the cold leather couch cushion.

"So then what's going on with you and your patient? I mean, I haven't seen him myself, but some of the other girls have. They sounded pretty jealous when they mentioned you've been visiting him during your breaks." I can hear her smiling through the phone.

I roll onto my back and rest my feet against the wall behind the couch. "Did they actually sound jealous?" I get caught up in her excitement.

"Ah, ah. Details first, and then I'll tell you what they said. Spill it," she demands.

"Okay, well, I visited Henry today, and things actually got pretty hot between us. We kissed, and Alexis walked in on us." I move the phone away from my ear, expecting Sheila to shriek.

"What the hell is going on?" she yells into the microphone. "How the hell did this all happen so fast?"

"Well, he and I have been talking non-stop since he first got admitted, and when he found out about Aiden and me, he kind of jumped at the opportunity. He was showing me his knee and saw me checking out his leg tats, and the next thing I know, he pulled me into a kiss." I giggle as I recall the moment, blushing like a schoolgirl.

"Honestly, Sheila, he's just so different than Aiden. I think I just want to spend my time with him for now and see what happens," I say gleefully.

"Well, I can't argue with that. I'm glad you're finally chasing what makes you happy." She yawns. "Alright, I need to go to sleep. I've been awake for way too long," she groans. "I better see you during my next lunch break. No more sneaking away."

"Okay, okay. I'll be waiting in the break room with two cups of coffee. Now, go get some rest. God knows I need to do the same." I hang up and use all the strength left in my body to lift myself off the couch. After walking around for twelve hours, it's hard to leave a comfortable spot like this, but I still need to clean off before I can climb into bed.

I exhale in disappointment and drag myself to the bathroom.

31

CHARLIE

SATURDAY, JUNE 23RD: 6:45 P.M.

A LITTLE BLUE bird sits perched on a branch outside my kitchen window, staring at me as I scramble some eggs. It's chirping as if trying to tell me something, but what? Maybe it's angry about my breakfast.

"Don't open the door," a man's voice whispers.

What? I look around frantically. Who the hell said that?

The bird's mouth opens again, and I step closer to the window to get a look at this magical bird when a loud knock startles us. I jump and the bird to flap its wings violently before flying away. My veins go ice cold in fear.

The door.

I tiptoe to the front of the house and peek through the peep hole. Three police officers are standing on the other side, hands at their weapons. *Oh my gosh, what the hell is going on?*

"Ma'am. Please open the door," one officer says in a polite, yet aggravated voice.

I open the door and peek through the crack. "Hello. Can I help you?" My knees tremble as I speak, so I grip the wall for support.

"Yes, you can." The first officer puts his large boot between the door and the frame so I can't close it. "You're under arrest for attempted murder." He shoves his way into the house, pushing me to the ground.

"Wait!" I scream. "I didn't do it, I swear!" I plead on my knees, begging for mercy.

"That's not what Aiden says." His figure grows into a giant as he speaks down at me, pinning me harder. He grabs me under my arms and lifts me to my feet. "Let's go," he says as he wraps cold metal cuffs around my wrists.

"No, this is a mistake! He's lying!" I shout as he drags me out of the house.

I lunge forward, drenched in sweat and out of breath. The room is spinning from how quickly I sat up. I look around and realize I'm sitting in bed—it was all a bad dream.

My head falls back into my sweat-drenched pillow, and I sigh in relief. This guilt is weighing on me more than I thought. The memory of that night grows heavier in my mind, especially now that I've gotten to know Henry. I feel like I'm betraying everyone who has ever put their trust in me.

I grab my phone from the nightstand to check for any messages and see one from Henry.

> Hey, I get released from the hospital today, so you won't be able to visit my room tonight as much as you may want to. ;)

My stomach is in knots after that dream. He's too good to be true, yet I'm keeping this horrible secret from him. There's only one way this story can end, and I'm terrified.

I throw my phone to the floor to keep myself from responding. I need to focus on myself right now. How can I possibly keep talking to him when I know everything will end in disaster? All I can do is go back to my regular life and pray my dream isn't actually a premonition.

I warily walk into my bathroom, still shaken from my nightmare, and look at myself in the brightly-lit mirror. *I look tired.* My dark hair is tangled on one side, eyes droopier than usual. I'm feeling burnt out from work and life in general; it's all beginning to feel like too much. It's like the world around me is caving in, and there's no way out of this hole.

I sit on the cold tile floor and allow the dark cloud in my chest to consume me.

The sound of my phone ringing pulls me out of my head. I don't feel like doing anything right now; I just want to go back to bed and sleep the night away like a normal person.

My body feels heavy as I slowly make my way over the phone, where Henry's name lights up my screen. I stare for a minute, debating what to do. Should I pick up?

No, no. You need to distance yourself from him. This whole situation is getting too messy, and I'm doing enough cleanup in my life as it is.

I hit 'ignore' and get ready for work. I need some time to think.

The house feels different when I come home from work. It's less cluttered than before. Not that our house is usually dirty, but it looks like small items have either been moved or taken. The decorative book from the coffee table is gone, and so are a couple of art pieces from the wall above the couch.

I cautiously walk into the bedroom to see if anything else is out of place and find a trail of hangers leading from the closet to the bed. Aiden's side has been completely emptied. I guess he found somewhere else to live.

I grab my phone and draft a text to him.

> Hey, I saw you took your things. Are you moving out or just going away for a few days?

My finger lingers over the screen for a moment before hitting send.

I knew we wouldn't live together after breaking up, but seeing his things gone make me realize how real this is. I can afford rent on my own, but it would be tight. I'll need to find a roommate until my lease ends.

Today is the end of my workweek, and I'm going to do everything in my power to clear my mind. I turn on the TV and go to the kitchen to pre-heat the oven. The log of chocolate chip cookie dough is calling my name, and I gladly oblige, scooping a spoonful into my mouth.

I slide the tray into the oven and take a bottle of wine with me to the couch. Tonight, no men, no negativity, no guilt. It's all about peace and relaxation. I mindlessly flip through the channels, trying to find something to watch, and land on our local news station, as if inviting in more stress.

I pour myself a glass of wine as my favorite weatherman goes over the forecast, predicting a monsoon to hit tomorrow morning. I have mixed feelings about monsoon season; on one hand, I get to enjoy rain and clouds, but on the other hand, my hair doesn't agree with the humidity. It's nice to watch from indoors, though, where I can cozy up with a book next to the window blasting the A.C. and pretend it's actually cold out.

I'll bet Henry loves the rain too. I mean, he grew up on the East Coast, where they have all four seasons. I've always wanted to visit the Big Apple, but I just never got around to it. I love to imagine myself visiting during fall, when I can enjoy hot coffee at some corner cafe as all the busy New Yorkers bustle past the window to their big office jobs. I'll bet the foliage is beautiful there too.

Henry probably wore various chic rain coats to work, ones that look sophisticated but not like he's trying too hard.

Wait, stop. Henry shouldn't be in my head right now. I need to focus on myself, so I shoo him out of my brain like a bee trapped inside a car. Out the window, you go.

I turn up the volume of the TV to hopefully silence all the chatter in my mind. The two news anchors are joking with one another about something that happened over the weekend. It's nice that they can get so personable on air like that. I enjoy watching the morning news because it's typically lighter stories, which I need, since my work is so heavy. All the death and illnesses can really make you feel depressed if you think about it enough, so this is usually a good change of pace.

"Okay, well, moving on. A local activist is raising money for a teacher who was the victim of a hit-and-run incident earlier this month," the news woman says. The wine nearly comes out of my nose as I grab the remote to increase the volume.

"Mayoral candidate John Whitman shared these images to his social media pages today, calling on the public for any information relating to the hit-and-run crash that left a beloved elementary school teacher hospitalized. In his post, he calls for anyone with information on the incident to contact police and asks those who want to help to donate to a fundraising page the victim's family set up to help cover medical expenses," the male anchor says, a brow raised.

I sit still for a moment, my mouth wide open as images of poor Henry fill my TV screen. When did this happen? So, Henry decided to talk to this guy after all? Thousands of thoughts come rushing into my mind, like a tidal wave of negativity. What does this mean for me? I can feel myself spiraling. *It doesn't matter Charlie,* I try to calm myself. *They still don't know anything. You retraced your steps. There were no cameras, no witnesses. No one can blame us for this.*

I'm clenching my fists so tight, my hands start to cramp. I'm so torn. I care about Henry so much, yet I'm keeping this terrible secret from him. God, what should I do? I drop to my knees in an act of desperation. "Please, God. I'm sorry for not praying to you more often. I'm sorry for not going to church, but please, send me a sign. I'm so lost right now." I drop my head on the coffee table and sob. I wish things were different. I wish I could go back in time and stop us from going to that bar. It wasn't worth it.

My phone vibrates on the table next to my head. *God?* I grab it quickly and check the screen, partly expecting a text from the man upstairs. It's Henry again.

> Hey, I'm sure you're asleep right now, but I wanted to thank you for keeping me company.

My heart skips a beat. Is this a sign? Maybe this is the universe telling me I can keep seeing Henry, and everything will be okay. Or maybe it's just my delusional brain telling me what I want to hear. The oven dings, and I jump up to take the cookies out of the oven. At the scent, I'm immediately transported to my version of heaven. I shove a hot, chewy bite into my mouth and feel just a tiny bit better—until the melted chocolate burns the roof of my mouth.

I pull up my phone again to text back.

> Hey, I'm not asleep yet. I just got home from work and wasn't tired. And of course, I wanted to make sure you were okay. I'm glad you're out now.

I swipe back over to Instagram and type in the name I just heard on the news. John Whitman. Like every other politician in America, his page is littered with photos of himself standing with 'regular' people. It seems this guy is really active within the teachers' union, which could be why he took a special interest in Henry's case. He pinned the photo I saw on TV at the top of his profile so it's the first post people see when they visit his page. I click on the image to find it already has more than 1,000 likes.

My finger lingers over the comment icon as I debate whether I want to subject myself to such cruelty. *I do.* I'm filled with regret almost immediately. Endless comments tag the police department, calling on them to do more, while others speculate about the horrible person responsible. I'm about thirty comments deep when a message from Henry pops up on my screen.

> Would you want to meet up outside the hospital sometime? Maybe you can come to my place for dinner. I may be in a wheelchair, but I can still cook.

The thought of him making me dinner and pouring me a glass of wine sends chills down my back. I know I should be avoiding him, but I can't resist.

> I'd like that. I'm going to bed now, so just text me the deets. It's the end of my work week, so I'm free for the next three days.

I'm going to regret this later. I walk into the room with a second cookie in my mouth, drop my clothes, and plop onto the bed. I didn't shower, but dizziness hits me like a ton of bricks. I don't think I have it in me to stay up much longer.

32

CHARLIE

SUNDAY, JUNE 24TH: 4:14 P.M.

THE AIR FEELS SWEETER TODAY. I walk outside with a fresh cup of coffee in hand to see large gray clouds forming just past the mountains in the distance. For a moment, I forget about all the shit that's happened, and I'm completely at peace.

Now is the perfect time for a run. I pull my hair back and toss on my running shoes while I still have this boost of energy. I've decided to change my attitude about this whole situation after a thought occurred to me last night. Worrying only makes you suffer twice. It's a good reminder to slow down and look at the big picture. I'm not dying, and it's not the end of the world. It's going to be okay—at least, that's what I try to convince myself. Maybe if I say it enough, I'll eventually believe it.

The air outside is hot and sticky from the storm that's rolling in. I hate the humidity, but I'd take this over the dry desert heat any day. At least I don't have the sun beating down on my back.

Sometimes, I forget how beautiful this neighborhood is. I take a moment to literally smell the roses as I jog past a luscious garden in someone's front yard. An elderly woman smiles and waves as she clips some rose bushes on the other side of her fenced-in lawn.

My muscles get warmer as I push harder against the sidewalk. Henry was running the night he got hit. Does he normally run at night like that? Is he normally up that late? I'm sure, as a teacher, he's usually up early for work, so what was he doing outside at that time anyway?

The thought gets my adrenaline going, and I'm now sprinting with all my might. My lungs are on fire, and there's the slight taste of blood in my mouth, but I keep going. The pain is welcome right now.

I don't let myself slow until I see my house in the distance. I pull my cell phone out of my pocket to check the time as I try to catch my breath and see another message from Henry.

> Are you doing anything tonight? I can make mushroom risotto.

I wipe the sweat from my brow as I walk back inside. *Dinner tonight?* It's already 4:30, and I still need to shower and get ready.

> What time were you thinking?

I reply.

I really would like more time to go shopping. I haven't been on a date in a long time and don't have any nice clothes.

> I've actually got some things to do today. Could we do tomorrow instead?

I text Sheila next; I'll need her help picking out something to wear.

> Hey, are you free tomorrow? I really need a girls' day.

I toss my phone on the bed and jump in the shower to wash this sweat away.

The house feels strange without Aiden here. Granted, our different schedules meant we were alone more than we were together, but still. I feel like he died and his spirit still wanders the halls.

I almost feel guilty reading the book Henry loaned me, as if Aiden's ghost is peering over my shoulder, judging me for moving on so soon, though I know in my heart, that's not true. I moved on long before the incident.

I'm about three quarters of the way through, and I'm captivated by his mother's writing. I've been on the edge of my seat all evening trying to finish, and I already know I want to read the next one in the series. I wonder what it was like to have such a powerful woman for a mother. Mine never did anything interesting, particularly with her struggle with depression. She didn't enjoy conversation, even with her own kids, and when she did speak, it was usually short and to the point. I imagine having a writer as a mother makes for an interesting childhood. She probably told Henry creative bedtime stories and showed him how to use his imagination.

I'm trying to finish her book before our date tomorrow so I can return it. Plus, it will give us something to talk about over dinner.

33

CHARLIE

MONDAY, JUNE 25TH: 2:45 P.M.

SHEILA TEXTS me to let me know she's waiting outside. I put on a thin layer of mascara and lip gloss, grab my bag, and run out the front door. "Hey!" I yell as I swing open the passenger door. "Thanks for hanging out with me today. I really need to get out for a while." I direct the air vents towards me as I adjust my seatbelt. The air outside is still gray and muggy from the monsoon. Raindrops trickle onto the windshield before turning into a full shower.

"Yeah, no problem. So dinner, huh? Where you guys going?" she asks, eyes glued to the road, but I can tell she's trying to hide a smile.

"Yeah, he invited me to his house for dinner, since he's temporarily in a wheelchair."

"Oh, my God, Charlie. You're going to his house? You know what that means, right?"

"Uh, that he's afraid of non-accessible restaurants?" I shrug.

"More like Bow Chicka Wow Wow." She laughs. "He's probably expecting sex!" she yells. "Are you ready for that?"

My mouth drops at the suggestion. Could she be right? No,

Henry's a gentleman. He's not the type to expect sex on the first date. *Especially in his condition.*

"Sheila, the man is literally in a wheelchair." I roll my eyes.

"His leg is broken, not his dick." She snorts as she pulls into the mall parking lot.

"Okay." She lets out a long sigh, mentally preparing herself to brave the storm outside. "You ready?" She flashes a mischievous grin.

"Go," I shout.

We swing open our doors simultaneously and run to the glass doors of the mall, squealing like children as we shield our faces from the down pour.

"Makeup was a mistake." Sheila pants as we enter the protection of the mall. "Anyway." She wipes her smudged eyes, trying to continue the conversation. "All I'm saying is, just be ready. That's all."

Could she be right? Oh God, I feel sick. I haven't been with anyone beside Aiden. I wouldn't know what to do. The thought alone makes me self-conscious, suddenly hyper-aware of every roll and dimple on my body.

Sheila can sense the alarm bells in my head and tries to calm me. "Then again, you're probably right. You know him better than I do, and he's probably just excited to see you without the puke-stained scrubs." She grabs my hand and guides me into the first store.

"Thanks, but you're right. I should be prepared, just in case. Last thing I want is him trying to undress me when I wasn't expecting it." I mentally add lingerie to the list of items to buy. None of my bras and panties match, and the ones I do own aren't anything special. Mainly sports bras and boy shorts, things I can comfortably work long shifts in.

"What should I wear then? I'm going to his house, so I don't want to look weird by dressing too fancy. Plus, with this weather,

I can't show too much skin without being obvious." I groan as I think aloud.

"Oh, what about this?" She pulls out a mid-thigh length black skirt with flower embellishments. "You can wear it with a cute long sleeve shirt or something." She hands it to me to try on.

"Really? With the rain? I won't look like I'm trying too hard?" I clutch the skirt to my chest.

"Babe, you're overthinking. Just wear black tights underneath. You're covered up, and I think it's sexier that way anyway." She winks. "Now, go try it on."

She was right to pick this. It hugs my hips just right, but is long enough to leave someone wanting more. I grab a simple black fitted long sleeve to go along with it and head out.

"I made us an appointment at Madelyn's to get our nails done," I say as we wander around the mall. "But it's not for another half hour, so should we go grab some coffee first?" I've only had one cup today, so I'm due for a pick-me-up. It's hard to be awake while the sun is out. Luckily, Sheila understands.

"Ugh, yes please. I'm in desperate need of some caffeine." We laugh as we get in line at a coffee shop a few doors down. It feels nice to have a day to ourselves like this, without the hustle and bustle of the hospital. I can feel myself slowly becoming more comfortable with this new life.

We get our usual drinks and walk to the salon. It feels like forever since I've treated myself like this. I don't usually get my nails done because of my job, but I'll never pass up on a pedicure and foot massage. Plus, I love keeping my toes pretty.

A small older woman with glasses and shoulder-length gray hair leads us to our seats.

"I'm really glad we're doing this, Charlie." Sheila looks at the pedicure options in front of her. "I'm glad you're finally figuring out what you want. Everyone deserves to be happy," she says as she points to the Deluxe Pedicure on the paper from the nail tech.

She's right. I do deserve to be happy. I lean back and turn on the massage chair, melting into my seat as it digs into the knots under my shoulder blades. "Thanks, Sheila. I know it seems like I'm moving fast, but—"

"Please! Aiden's the one moving fast. He literally kissed another woman while you were still together. I'll bet they fucked less than 24 hours after you dumped him," she interrupts. The women massaging our feet peek up with raised eyebrows, as if intrigued by the gossip before them, though I'm sure they've heard way worse on the job.

"Huh. Yeah, you're right." I close my eyes and try to focus on the movements of the nail tech's hands. Her thumbs are hitting all the right places on my foot, and I swear, I nearly purr like a kitten. As someone who works on her feet all day, I should really start treating myself to pedicures more often. Maybe it will help with my mood.

"God, I need to do this more often," I moan.

"Wait. Charlie, look!" Sheila shouts.

I open my eyes, and she's pointing ahead at the TV on the wall. "I think that's about Henry," she says.

My mouth drops as I try to listen to what they're saying. The banner at the bottom of the screen says, *Police Release Image Of Car Involved in Hit-and-Run of Local Teacher.*

"Wow, that's good..." Sheila's voice fades into the background as I try to focus on the photo. My heart sinks as I stare at a grainy image of Aiden's car. Where was this photo taken? I retraced our steps and know there were no street cams. This looks like it could have been a doorbell camera, but the quality is very poor, too pixelated to get an exact make or model. The only thing you can tell for sure is that it's a dark colored sedan, which isn't rare in this community.

"Hey." Sheila waves her hand next to my face. "Charlie, are you okay?"

"Uh, yeah. I'm fine." I nod my head. "I was just thinking about Henry and what he thinks about all of this." I sigh. Maybe tonight isn't a good idea after all.

"Well, it's a good thing you're seeing him tonight then," she says, as if reading my thoughts. "You'll be able to help get his mind off things." She leans back in her chair.

I know Aiden isn't talking to me, but this is something he should know about. Right? I pull out my phone and try finding the news article online. Several links appear with images. I close my eyes and try to calm myself before continuing. Nausea is brewing in my stomach, and I don't know how I'm going to eat dinner tonight. I tap the first article and send the link to Aiden. Who knows if he's going to open it, but it's worth a shot.

34

CHARLIE

MONDAY, JUNE 25TH: 7:35 P.M.

I STARE at myself in the mirror, closely examining every pore and dry patch on my face. My nerves are still a wreck, and I'm supposed to be at Henry's house in the next thirty minutes. *Get it together, Charlie.* You're about to meet a smart, sexy man for dinner; things could be worse. I perk up, put on my hot girl playlist to boost my spirits, and get ready.

Tonight seems like a good time for fiery red lipstick. It shows off the round shape of my lips and matches the embroidered flowers on my skirt. I lightly fluff my dark eyebrows and put on mascara and a light layer of blush. I don't usually wear foundation, because I can never find a shade that looks right on my skin.

I send a cute selfie to Sheila and head out the door, trying my best not to throw up from the anxiety. This is the first time I'm having dinner with a man who's not related or engaged to me, and, honestly, I'm nervous.

Things felt more natural in the hospital room. I don't know if it's because I was in my element or maybe because he was bedbound, but tonight is different. I'll be in his element, his home. I tighten my grip on the steering wheel as I think of potential conversation starters.

I look to the right, where his mother's book peeks through from under my purse. The book. Yes, we can talk about that when I give it back to him.

I pull into a gated community, lined with townhomes that look exactly the same. I'm trying to find Henry's, but I think I'm lost. This neighborhood feels like a maze.

Finally, I see his house number and pull into the driveway.

Okay, Charlie. It's okay. It's just dinner, I try to convince myself. I readjust my breasts so they're perky like God intended, grab my things, and head for the front door.

A few moths circle the patio light above me as I wait for him to answer. The gold knob starts jingling, and I immediately fix my posture. It creeks open to expose a beautiful woman with hazel eyes and fluffy, light brown hair. "Hi, you must be Charlie." She smiles wide as she pulls me in for a hug.

"Uh, hi. Yes, I am." I reluctantly pat her on the back. "And you are?" I cock my head.

"Ugh, Henry! Did you forget to tell her I was visiting?" she yells toward the kitchen. "I'm Avery, his older sister. I'm visiting from London until he can take care of himself," she jokes. "Come, come. Dinner's almost ready." She grabs my hand and pulls me into the kitchen. Her skin is as soft as lotion. "Can I get you a glass of wine?" She starts opening a bottle of Sangiovese.

"Uh, yeah. That would be nice. Thanks." I look around the room for Henry, but he's nowhere in sight. His place is nice, though, very warm and welcoming. It's just as chic as I had imagined. The dark wood shelves in his living room are lined with colorful books, creating a beautiful and catalogue-like contrast. Tasteful art also covers the walls, and several oriental rugs line the floors.

"Here you go," she interrupts my thoughts. "I'm sorry if I took you by surprise, but I was just so excited to meet the woman who saved my baby brother." Her eyes well up with tears as she looks at me. "I'm really grateful for you." She puts the glass to her lips and takes a large gulp.

"Speaking of your brother, where is he?" I try to sound casual and not at all uncomfortable.

"Oh, he spilled some sauce on his shirt right before you got here, so he went to change. He should be right back." She turns her attention to the stove to stir the food in the pot.

I pull my phone out while her attention is away and text Sheila. "Omg, I was so wrong. Not a date. His sister is here!" I hit send and immediately slide my phone back into my bag.

I stand and walk into his living room, examining the art on the wall. A lot of these photos are vintage illustrations from famous books, like *Treasure Island*, *The Great Gatsby*, *To Kill a Mockingbird*. He's really passionate about literature.

"Hey there," a smooth voice sounds from behind me.

"Oh, hey!" I turn around. He's standing! "What happened to the wheelchair?" I ask.

He has a suspicious smile on his face, as if he caught me talking to myself but is too polite to say anything. "Well, the doctors said I could switch between the chair and crutches." I'm a little stunned by his height, since I've only seen him in bed. He's at least a foot taller than me, strong in stature but not too bulky.

"I'm glad you could make it. I see you've already met my sister." He flashes a look at her over his shoulder. "Can I get you anything to drink? I'm about to serve up dinner." His voice is so deep and calm.

"Thank you, but Avery already poured me a glass." I smile in her direction. From the corner of my eye, I see Henry grab his phone to quickly send a message before sliding it back into his pocket. His sister's cell phone buzzes on the counter next to her, and her eyes pop open.

"Well, I have a lot of work to catch up on, and I should probably give Dave and the kids a call. I'm just going to take some of this and go to my room." She smiles as she plops a generous serving of risotto into her bowl before she scurries into the guest bedroom.

"Goodnight!" Henry and I say simultaneously. We giggle as we make our way back to the kitchen. I feel like a high schooler again, trying to keep our parents from seeing us together.

"I like your sister. She's got spunk," I say as I take a seat at the kitchen counter.

"That she does." He smiles as he turns his attention to the food. "You wanna take a seat at the table? I can bring you your food."

"Are you sure? Do you need any help?" I offer.

"No, no. I got it." He winks. "Just go take a seat."

He carries two dishes on one arm as he balances with his crutch in the other and sets a plate in front of me that looks like it came straight from a restaurant. Mushroom risotto with parmesan cheese on top.

He smiles as he sets down two glasses of wine. "By the way, you were right the first time." He looks like he's holding back laughter as he takes a seat across from me.

"Right about what?" I ask.

"This definitely *is* a date. My sister being here was a surprise for both of us." He laughs as he shoves a bite into his mouth.

What is he talking about? *Oh no.* I pull out my phone to see I texted Henry instead of Sheila and slide down my chair in embarrassment. "I'm so sorry. I didn't mean to send that to you." I cover my face with my hands and feel my skin get warmer.

"It's okay." He laughs. "Really. I'm sorry for surprising you like that. I'm sure you weren't expecting a woman to answer the door."

"No problem," I lie as I stuff a spoonful of risotto into my mouth. My embarrassment melts away almost immediately as buttery mushroom and parmesan coat my mouth. "Wow, this is really good," I say as I go in for another bite.

"Oh, before I forget—I finished your book." I grab it from my bag. "Here you go." I get a whiff of his musky scent as I hand it to him.

"Oh yeah? How did you like it?" He smiles as he looks deeply into my eyes. I quickly look at my glass of wine to avoid his stare.

"Yeah, it was good. I definitely want to read the other two." I take another bite of risotto.

"Well, I have them here if you want to borrow them." He points to his built-in bookshelf in the living room.

"You read a lot. I'm impressed," I say.

"Were all of your exes illiterate?" he teases.

I roll my eyes and smile. "Something like that."

Henry clears his throat. "You're beautiful. You know that?" He swirls the wine in his glass before taking a sip.

"Thank you," I reply. I look at his crutches leaning against his chair and am suddenly consumed with guilt and embarrassment. He has no idea the woman sitting across from him, eating his food and chatting with his sister, was involved in the crash that put him here. I'm a fraud, like one of those women who swindles their way into a man's life and cons him out of his life savings. For some reason, hiding from the police feels easier than lying to him.

"Can I see the rest of the series?" I ask, trying to take the attention off myself.

He looks at me for a moment with slanted eyes, as if trying to read my mind. "Yeah of course." He stands, book still in hand, and grabs his crutches. "Follow me," he instructs.

I do as I'm told and follow him into the living room, where various titles line the dark shelves. He goes straight to the far left shelf and pulls two books from the top row, sliding the book I just returned into its place. He must have his library memorized. "Here you go." He smiles.

I grab the books from his hand and look at the covers. They're just as beautiful as the first one. It must be interesting for him to see his mother's name on his shelf like this.

"Thanks," I say. "I'm excited to read them."

"I'm eager to hear how you like them. Don't hold back just because I'm the author's son."

"Are we starting a book club?" I joke.

"I'm not opposed. The two of us? Maybe the nurse who walked in on us the other day? Can you think of anyone else we should invite?"

I let out a weak laugh. "Can I ask you something?"

I can tell I piqued his interest. "Yeah, shoot."

"Why did you invite me here tonight?" I look at him as he ponders the question.

"Because I like you," he states matter-of-factly. "Why do you ask?"

"But why do you like me? You don't even know me, and I'm not as good as you think." I pull a random book from the shelf and examine the cover to avoid his curious gaze.

He lets out a loud laugh. "Good. Neither am I," he says as he gently grabs the book from my hand, sliding it back into its spot. He's so close, I can feel his body heat radiating onto me. His gray cotton shirt hugs his hard-earned muscles perfectly.

I look up at the man towering before me, my face is only chest-level.

"No one is completely good." He steps closer, cupping my face in his large, calloused hand, my back now pressed against the bookcase. The shelves are stabbing my spine, but I don't care. His hand tightens around my face, pulling me in for a kiss. His firm body presses into mine. I'm not sure what I was expecting him to say, but it definitely wasn't this.

I wrap my arms around his neck, intertwining my fingers. He scoops his hands under my butt and stands straight, lifting me off the ground. "What about your leg?" I gasp.

"Don't worry about me." He shoves his tongue back into my mouth and my back into the books behind me. He moves his mouth to my neck, kissing along my collar bone, working his way up to my earlobe.

"Actually," he grunts in pain, "my leg isn't quite ready for that after all." He blushes as he sets me back down. He grabs my hand instead and guides me to his room. I toss the books he handed me onto the couch before following.

"Sit down," he demands, pointing to the neatly made bed in the center of the room. His sheer presence makes my body vibrate with excitement. He whips off his shirt, exposing his tan, firm stomach and well-maintained chest hair. He sits on the bed next to me, lifts my body again, and sets me on his lap. His sheer strength is astonishing.

"Get undressed," he huffs. I can't help but do as he tells me. Thank God Sheila and I went shopping earlier. I drop my top, showcasing my new emerald green lace bra that cups my breasts perfectly. He scoops them into his hands and groans. "God, your body is perfect," he says as he shoves his face into my chest, inhaling deeply, as if to memorize my scent. My body quivers as he gently bites the top of my breast.

Now it's my turn to take the lead.

I push his shoulders back so he lays flat on the bed. "Is your leg still okay?" I ask, scared my body weight may hurt him.

"Stop worrying about me." He grunts as I run my fingers across his stomach and through his chest hair. He relaxes, allowing me to kiss his chest, running my lips across his neck, ears, then mouth. His lips welcome mine in a tender embrace, as if we'd haven't seen each other in years, full of yearning.

He unhooks my bra and lifts my skirt to my stomach. "Are these expensive?" he asks as he grips my black nylon tights.

"No," I say.

"Good." He rips them open at the seam, grabs me by the hips, and pulls me over his face.

35

AIDEN

MONDAY, JUNE 25TH: 11:32 P.M.

I'M SCROLLING through apartment listings on my laptop as Lexi cooks up a late-night snack. She's been letting me crash here until I find a new place to live. I like her, but I think this whole situation has given her the wrong impression.

"Here you go." She hands me a plate with half a ham sandwich before she sits on the cushion next to me.

"Thanks," I grunt.

"Any luck?"

"Not really. A lot of these places look shitty, and the ones that are decent go quick," I complain.

"Well, you can stay with me as long as you need." She kisses me on the cheek and leans back so she can tune in to her medical drama on TV. Of course she watches the only show that reminds me of Charlie.

I try my best to pay attention to my computer. The text message notification sits at the bottom of my screen, showing me I have several unread messages. Three are from Charlie, but I've been avoiding opening them. Nothing she has to say will make me feel better. She made her bed; now, she has to lay in it.

I look over at Lexi, whose bright eyes are glued to the

screen, then back at the text message icon. I should just get this over with so the notification stops taunting me. I click her name and see two messages, plus a link to some news article. It's a story about the accident. *Shit*. They have a photo from that fucking night! That's my fucking car on the screen!

I enlarge the image and stare closely. It looks pretty grainy, and I can hardly make out the model or even color of the car. You can tell it's a dark sedan, but that's about it. I don't even see a license plate. I examine the surroundings to try and figure out where this image was taken; it looks like it was right before that corner where I hit the runner.

I slam my laptop shut and sit back. What the fuck am I going to do? Luckily, the image isn't super clear, but still. They're bound to figure out what happened. I aggressively rub my sweaty hands on my knees.

"Aiden?" a gentle voice pulls me from my manic thoughts.

"Huh?" I manage to force out.

"Is something wrong?" She leans in, rubbing my arm. "What were you just looking at?"

"Oh, uh, nothing. Sorry, I guess I'm getting a little over-whelmed with this apartment hunt. It's different now that I'm on a single income." I manage to fake a laugh. "It's going to be an adjustment, that's all." I grab the sandwich and shove a big bite into my mouth to avoid answering more questions.

"I'm sorry. I'm sure that's very stressful. Just remember, you made the right choice leaving her if you weren't happy." She scoots closer and wraps her dainty arms around my chest, trying but failing to completely reach around me.

"Yeah, you're right," I mumble, my mouth full as I stare miserably at the TV screen.

Things used to be so good; how did this happen? We had our routine. We knew each other better than anyone else. How could she just throw it all away like that? How could she be so heartless? What happened to for better or worse?

And now, the fucking cops are going to arrest me. . I imagine this is what it feels like to get hit by a bus. Maybe that would actually be better.

I really don't want to see her, but maybe it's time Charlie and I had a talk.

36

CHARLIE

TUESDAY, JUNE 26TH: 2:15 A.M.

I LIE IN BED, wrapped in Henry's warm arms, while the storm rages outside. The room is dark, and all I can see are the gray outlines of his furniture. I can't believe that just happened. My heart is still racing.

Henry groans and pulls me in tighter, squeezing me like a stuffed animal. I bury my face into his bare chest, inhaling the savory scent of his skin, and I can't help but smile.

"I wish we could lay like this forever," I whisper.

"That'd be nice." He gently kisses the top of my head. "Can I ask you something?"

"Of course." A hint of worry settles in the pit of my stomach.

"I feel like you know a lot more about me than I know about you." He releases me so he can see my face. "I'd like to learn more. Where did you grow up?" His dark eyes glimmer under the faint moonlight peeking through the window shades.

"I'm from a small beach town outside of San Diego." Relief washes over me.

"Ah, a beach girl." He smiles. "Why would you leave the ocean for a desolate place like Redwell?" He furrows his dark brows.

"Desolate?" I laugh. "This place isn't *that* bad."

I let out a long sigh and roll onto my back. The large metal ceiling fan spins silently and effortlessly above us, unlike the dusty old one at my place. "I originally came here for school because it was far from home but still close enough for a weekend visit. I'm now just trying to get some real work experience under my belt before going back home, since the job market there is so competitive."

"Beautiful and career-oriented," he says. "Can I ask you another question?"

"You don't need permission," I laugh. "Ask away."

"Okay." He pauses. "What happened between you and your ex?"

I should have expected this question at some point. My chest tightens as I try to pinpoint exactly what went wrong with Aiden. It's more than just the accident. It was one issue after the other, like a row of dominoes knocking over the pillars of our relationship until there was nothing left to hold us up.

"Um..." I try to gather my thoughts. "As cliché as this sounds, I guess we just grew apart," I say. "Our schedules never aligned, so we hardly had time together and when we did, we usually fought. Aiden started getting angry with the world, focusing on the things he didn't have or only pointing out things that are wrong. It just turned into a really negative dynamic."

"Hm." Henry nods. "I can understand why you would want to leave."

"Yeah. When I found out he fooled around with his co-worker, I knew our relationship was over because I didn't care that he cheated," I admit.

Henry pulls me back into his arms for a tight embrace. "I'm sorry, Charlie."

"It's okay." I set my face on his chest. "It led me here."

I open my eyes, momentarily panicking as I forget where I am.

That's right—I'm in his bedroom. *Henry's bedroom*, I remind myself. I smile as I look next to me, only to realize I'm alone in bed. He must have stepped out so I could sleep in.

I sit up and stretch my arms as I look around. His room looks much different in the daylight. It has a lot of the same personality as his living room. I would describe the look as organized chaos, cluttered with various knickknacks, each neatly tucked into their own special place.

The bed creaks as I swing my legs over the edge, giving the rest of my body a moment to wake up. The bedroom door cracks open. "Oh, good. You're awake," Henry says as he pushes it open with his crutch, wooden tray in hand.

"What's this?" I smile.

"Just some coffee and croissants." He smiles as he wobbles to the bed, only one crutch supporting his recovering knee.

"I should be the one taking care of you. You need to rest that leg of yours, especially after last night," I laugh.

"You're probably right, but don't worry. My sister made the coffee and brought the pastries. I'm just bringing you some." He smiles. "How'd you sleep?" He sets the tray on the bed beside me.

"Great. Did you know you snore?" I laugh.

"Oh, really? Well, that makes two of us." He winks.

"What? I don't snore!" I playfully smack his arm.

"Hey, hey, don't shoot the messenger." He lifts his hands to surrender. "Anyway, I think it's cute." He tears off the corner of a croissant and stuffs it in his mouth. "Come out to the living room with us." He smiles and tosses me one of his shirts to put on.

"Thanks," I say as I slide it on, not bothering to find my bra first. The distressed black tee drapes over my body like a short dress, and I love the way it feels against my skin. *I'm wearing his shirt.* I jump up from the bed and follow him out of the room, my croissant and coffee in-hand.

"She's awake!" Avery announces from the couch. "How'd you sleep?" She tries to hide her smirk after seeing my attire.

"Good morning." I wince at the bright gray light shining through the skylight. "What time is it?" I look around the room for a clock.

"Just about noon." She smiles. "Henry says you're an overnight nurse, so this is usually your bedtime, huh? I get it. I'm usually asleep at this time too." She takes another gulp of coffee. "But mine is just jet lag. I can't imagine being completely nocturnal like you."

"Yeah, it can be challenging at times, lonely, especially since normal people are asleep when I'm up." I sit cross-legged in the lounge chair next to the couch.

"So...what took you to London?" I take a sip from the dark blue mug in my hands.

She smiles, as if recalling a distant happy memory. "Well, I went there for an externship and stayed because I met my husband. It's been about eight lovely years now." She looks longingly at Henry. "I've been trying to get baby Henry to apply to jobs out there so he could be closer to us, but so far, no luck." She pouts.

"Why wouldn't you want to go to London?" I look in his direction.

He rubs his arm. "Eh, I wasn't ready to leave then. But who knows? Things change." He takes a seat on the couch next to his sister. The slightest suggestion he could move is enough to appease her. It's nice to see their relationship up close.

"Why do you call him baby Henry?" I ask.

"Oh, well, that's because Henry was also our father's name.

That's just something us older folks started calling him to differentiate." She pulls her phone from her back pocket.

"I actually think I have some photos around here of the two of them. Dad's genes run strong in this one." She laughs as she scrolls through the images.

"Avery, no. I'm sure she doesn't want to look at old photos right now." He blushes.

"Well, I'm sure I *do* want to see some old photos. Bring 'em out!" I jump out of my chair and plop into the cushion next to this fiery woman.

"Oh, here we go!" she shouts. "I was looking through old photos recently and took pictures to email to family. Here's one of baby Henry and our dad." She hands me the phone. Henry, who looks about four, has a bowl cut and is sitting on his father's lap in a pair of tidy whiteys. His dad has a big beard, wears an 80s-looking suit, and has thick-lensed glasses perched on his nose. She was right—their faces look very similar, the only difference being his father was a little heavier with a lot more hair.

"That's so sweet." I hand her back the phone.

"Oh," Avery remembers, "and here's one of the whole family. This is our mother." Her eyes glisten as she looks longingly at the image.

"Avery..." Henry loses his smile. You can tell this is a sensitive topic, and he doesn't want his sister diving too deep into the matter. I wonder why.

"I'm sorry, Henry, but just look how happy she looked here." She hands him the phone to show him the image. It's a snapshot of the whole family in the kitchen. Baby Henry sits on the kitchen table in his underwear, eating scrambled eggs while his sister hugs their mother from behind as she washes dishes. Their father sits at the table next to him, a newspaper and coffee in hand.

Henry stares longingly at the screen for a moment before handing it back to her, a hint of sadness in his eyes. "You're right." His voice softens. "Can you send that to me?"

She smiles and gently pats him on the back. "Sure." She smiles.

"Our mom has Alzheimer's and lives in an assisted living facility in upstate New York," his sister explains.

Henry looks away, obviously uncomfortable with the topic.

"Oh, I'm so sorry," I say.

"It's okay." She smiles softly. "Well, I have to jump on an important video call in about ten minutes, so I'm going to run to the bathroom to freshen up my face." She rubs her hands on her knees as she stands.

"Oh really? We can head out if you need a quiet space to work," Henry suggests.

"Please, this is your house! I can't just kick you out." She laughs.

Henry grabs his crutch and pulls himself up. "No, no. I need some fresh air anyway. Charlie, how about it?" He looks at me with desperation in his eyes, obviously eager to get away from this trip down memory lane.

"Yeah, sure. Can we swing by my place first? I'd like to change out of these clothes," I suggest.

"Yeah, no problem." He holds out his hand to pull me up from the couch. "See ya later," he says to his sister.

37

———

HENRY

TUESDAY, JUNE 26TH: 12:30 P.M.

CHARLIE IS TAKING a long detour to her house to avoid driving down *that* street, obviously avoiding it for my sake. I pretend not to notice—I don't like lingering in the past anyway.

We pull into the driveway of a typical Arizona house, tan in color, with rocks in the front yard instead of grass.

"Okay, I just want to run in real quick and shower." She pops out of the car and runs to the passenger side to help me out like I'm crippled or something.

"Oh, I'm good. Thanks," I say as I hop out and grab my crutches from the backseat. My knee aches as I get out, but I don't tell her that, especially after she warned me so many times to take it easy last night. The pain was well worth it, though, and I would do it all over again just to feel her close. The smell of her skin is intoxicating and still lingers on my face.

"Okay." She smiles as she leads me to the front door. "I'm going to get ready. Feel free to just hang out. If you need anything to drink, the cups are in that cabinet, and there's some juice in the fridge." She bounces away.

"Take your time." I wave her off and make my way into the kitchen. The place is definitely messier than mine, but I wouldn't call it dirty. I open the cabinet she pointed to and see about a dozen mugs with different cartoons on them and only three regular mis-matched glasses.

I fill a Garfield-themed mug that says 'I Hate Mondays' with sink water and walk into the living room, just taking in my surroundings. I'm in her element right now, and it's exciting. I hear the shower turn on and remember the Charlie I saw last night—the curve of her hips and legs, the way her skin glistened under the strips of moonlight through the window shades. I need to experience that again.

Stop, Henry. I shake the thoughts from my head. *Don't get yourself excited now.*

I walk over to the couch covered in bright-colored blankets and pillows and take a seat. The place is emptier than I pictured. I would have guessed she just moved in. But then again, she did just go through a breakup, so maybe that's why. I wonder what her ex looks like.

I stand up and walk around, looking for any sign of him.

Who is he? What was he like? What was their relationship like? I have a bunch of questions, but I don't know if she'll be ready to answer them yet. For now, I'll have to settle for clues.

I reach the entertainment center, under the TV, and see a partially open drawer. Inside is a small framed photo of her with who I assume is her ex-fiancé. He has dirty blond hair and rosy pink cheeks. He looks like a frat boy who uses 'bro' every other sentence.

I hear the water turn off and quickly slide the photo back into its home before I hobble to the couch. The cold leather feels good against my skin.

"Hey." Charlie walks out in pants and a tee shirt, hair still wet and tangled. She grabs a hairbrush off the kitchen counter and starts brushing her hair next to me, flicking small specks of water onto my shoulder. "Do any good snooping?" She smiles as she violently strokes the brush against her head.

"I couldn't find anything good," I partially joke. Her natural face is beautiful and emulates genuine joy and warmth. It makes me want to curl up in her arms and fall asleep nuzzled in her chest again.

"So, what did you want to do today?" she asks, tucking dark damp strands of hair behind her ears, the ends leaving wet spots on her shirt.

"Um, I'm not sure," I say as I stand. The crutch acts as a ladder as I pull myself to my feet. I limp over to her gallery wall and pretend to look at the photos for the first time. "Is this your family?"

She comes to my side to examine the photo on the wall. "Yeah, that's my mom and sisters. We were visiting family in Florida there." She smiles. She smells incredible. I don't recognize the scent, but it's sweet and refreshing. It's hard to contain myself when she's this close to me. I just want to bury my face in her neck and breathe her in.

"You smell good." I smile at her.

"Thanks. It's my shampoo." She holds up a handful of her hair so I can get a better whiff.

"Yes," I laugh, "it's definitely your shampoo." I grab her by the hips and pull closer to me. "You're incredible." I look into her eyes, but she immediately looks away when I compliment her, as if praise makes her uncomfortable.

"What makes you say that?" She scoffs.

"Because you are." I gently lift her chin and kiss her lips. She looks at me with big doe eyes and then kisses me back. I hold her close to me, and for a moment, everything feels fine. I forget about getting hit, about being forced to leave work, about all the pain of leaving Mom behind. All this fucking shit seems to disappear when I'm with her.

"Henry." She looks to me like she needs to get something off her chest. "I-"

She's interrupted by the sound of the front door opening. Her eyes shoot open, like she realized she left the stove on. Our heads to turn to find a guy in dress pants and a button-up long-sleeve shirt standing in the doorway. He freezes like a deer in headlights with a betrayed look on his face. Based on the photo I saw earlier, he's the ex. But why is he walking in like he still lives here?

"Oh, uh, I didn't realize you had company." He stands still, unsure of what to do with himself.

"Aiden." She pushes away from me. "What are you doing here?"

"Well, my name is still on the lease, so I'm pretty sure I can come by whenever I want." He glares at me and then looks down at my knee brace. I can see his face change from angry to confused. He looks back to Charlie, as if to confirm what he's seeing. "I'll come back later." He turns away and slams the door shut behind him, rocking a couple of nearby picture frames on the wall.

Tears gloss over Charlie's eyes as she stares off into the distance. Am I missing something here? "Uh..." My words get trapped in my throat.

"I'm so sorry about that. Aiden and I don't speak. I have no idea why he showed up unannounced like that." She obviously sees the strange look on my face. "I mean, there is literally nothing between us anymore. That's why we broke up; plus, he already moved on. He got with his coworker while we were still together." She stumbles over her words as she tries to reassure me. This is obviously really stressful for her. I can't imagine having one of my exes barging in on me like that, especially in front of Charlie.

I take a deep breath and exhale like they teach in yoga

before responding. "It's okay." I bring her in for a hug, giving her the benefit of the doubt. "I get it. It's not like you invited him over." I try to calm her down. "But why did he say he would come back later?"

She leans back to look me in the eye. "I'm really not sure. I'm guessing he wanted to talk and clear the air. I mean, he has been avoiding me since we ended things. I've tried apologizing and making sure we end on good terms, but he never responded to any of my messages." Her eyes fall to the floor like a sad puppy. I really want to know more about this but don't want to push her too much. She's in a vulnerable place right now, and I don't want to make her cry more.

"Okay," I say. "How about we get out of here and get our mind off things? You're ready to go now, right?"

"Yeah, I'm ready," she sighs. "Fresh air will be good."

38

CHARLIE
TUESDAY, JUNE 26TH: 2:00 P.M.

I PULL into the parking lot of a nearby park. It features a man-made dirt path that branches out into various walking trails, like the root system of a tree. Each path is lined with various desert plants, accompanied by educational plaques about the vegetation. It's enough to make you feel like you're hiking without physically exerting yourself.

I don't come here often because of the heat, but this weather is providing a cool cover from the sun. It's still warm out, but it's more manageable.

"Huh. I've never been here before." Henry looks out the car window, taking in the landscape.

"Yeah." I pull into a parking space near the front. "It's nice. I like this spot because of all the plants. My family has a large garden back home, so I miss being around greenery, even though most of these plants are brown." I laugh.

"Come on," I say as I swing open the driver's side door. He follows behind me to a cement bench at the start of the trail.

I take a deep breath, the smell of wet earth from last night's rain filling my lungs. Small birds hop between branches of a bush ahead of us while a couple of small lizards nap on top of a large rock. "It's so nice out," I say.

"Do you ever think about moving back home?" Henry asks after a few minutes of silence.

I let out a long sigh. "Well, to be honest, it didn't feel like an option before. But with Aiden gone, maybe." My throat burns. "I really miss my family."

"Yeah, I feel that." He looks longingly into the distance. "It's hard not having them around, huh? Lonely."

"Can I ask you something?" I approach cautiously.

"Yeah, of course," he replies.

"You said you left New York because you needed a change in scenery. Why?" I don't shy away from his eyes like I normally do as I ask.

"Well," he clears his throat, "for the last couple of years, I have been my mother's caretaker. You know, Avery was in the U.K., and our father passed a few years back, so I was the only one left to help her when she first got diagnosed." His cheeks flex as he clenches his jaw. "It finally got too hard for me to manage by myself, so Avery and I checked her into a live-in care facility, where she can have around-the-clock medical attention. It's to the point that I can't even visit her; she thinks I'm my father and starts throwing stuff. I'm not even sure why. They had a happy marriage as far as I knew." He scratches his head. "So, I applied to teaching jobs all over the country, not really giving much thought to the location, and took the first offer I got."

My heart aches for him. I can't imagine the pain a decision like that brings. I'm sure it wasn't easy. A dark cloud forms in my chest as I look at his distant eyes. I wrap my arms around him and pull his big body into a hug.

"It's okay. I'm fine." He pulls away a little bit.

"Okay." I slide back to my side of the bench, trying to ignore the sting of his minor rejection.

"I'm sorry," he says. "I'm just—"

"It's okay," I interrupt. "You don't need to explain yourself."

He looks up at me with soft eyes. "Thank you." He leans back in and kisses me. The storm clouds in my chest evaporate, replaced with beams of sunlight.

39

CHARLIE

TUESDAY, JUNE 26TH: 4:00 P.M.

I DROPPED Henry off at his townhouse a little while ago and already miss him. I wish I was back in his arms instead of my cold, depressing bedroom.

He did his best to get my mind off Aiden earlier, but I can't help but feel an impending sense of doom. What the hell was so important that Aiden had to rush in like that? I feel physically and mentally drained and need some rest.

I crawl into my disheveled bed, nuzzle up with my plush pillows, and drift away.

The sound of my bedroom door clicking shut startles me awake. I sit forward to find a tall, dark figure standing at the foot of my bed. "What the fuck?" I screech as I yank my feet to my chest and out of their reach.

"Your boyfriend left, huh?" Aiden sits down on the edge of my mattress, giving me a closer look at his face. I turn on my bedside lamp to find him staring at me, cold and expressionless.

I scoot myself closer to the headboard to create some distance between us. "You don't knock anymore?"

"Well my—"

"And don't fucking say your name is on the lease. You took your things to God knows where and chose not to come home. We're broken up now, so that means you knock. It's just common decency," I snap.

"Please! Don't preach about common decency when you're the one who brought another man into our bed," he barks.

I can't help but laugh. "Yeah, well, at least I waited until *after* we were broken up." I roll my eyes.

He winces. "Look," he exhales, "I'm sorry she kissed me, but it wasn't my fault. What *you're* doing is on purpose."

"Oh, please. I know you were into it," I crack.

I know he's flustered when he starts to stutter. "I-I have no idea what you're talking about. You're fucking crazy." He jumps off the bed, offended by my accusation. "You're just making shit up now. Typical Charlie, trying to paint me as the bad guy when you're the one who chose to break up." His voice cracks in frustration.

"Whatever, Aiden. What do you want? Why did you come here?" There's no point in bringing up Lexi again, since he'll just lie the whole time anyway. Plus, I really don't care who he chooses to fuck.

"Look," he says sternly as he rubs his temples. "Just answer one question." He steps closer to my side of the bed, as if to assert dominance by towering over me. "Is the guy here earlier that jogger we hit?"

I open my mouth to speak, but my throat is nailed shut. "Uh," I let out. "Well, yes. I-I didn't want you to find out that way," I stutter as I slide out of bed to shorten the height gap between us.

"I knew I recognized him! His face is all over the fucking

news. What the hell, Charlie!" he shouts. "Now we're gonna go to jail because you couldn't keep your legs shut!" His face goes bright red.

"No. If we go to jail, it's because *you* ran him over with your car," I correct him.

He clenches his jaw so tightly, I can practically hear his molars cracking from the pressure. "Look, we need to figure out what we're going to do here," he says between his teeth, lips still stiff. "We're both to blame for this. You lied to the cops too, you know," he reminds me.

I can't believe this right now. Am I to blame? He's the one who wanted to drive us home and refused to slow the car when I said he was going too fast. He's the one who cut me off to lie to the cops because he didn't want to get in trouble. He's just full of bullshit, as usual. My body is now trembling in anger, and I can hardly speak.

"You wasted your time coming here since there's nothing to do. We can only wait it out," I say. "Now, please leave." I gesture to the bedroom door.

He shoves his hands in his pockets as he turns away. "You know, I wonder." He stops in his tracks. "How do you think your little boyfriend will react when he finds out your entire relationship is based on a lie? That you're not actually the hero he thought you were?" He rolls his eyes. "What you're doing to him is much worse than anything I could have done." He scoffs as he leaves the room, and my shoulders relax as soon as the front door slams shut.

The silence in the house is heavy, like a thick fog. He's right. What am I doing? Why am I wasting his time? Why did I start this with Henry knowing it'll destroy him in the end? Aiden's words echo in my brain like a scratched disk. This is going to blow up in my face, I can feel it.

I'm going to be sick.

I sprint to the bathroom and vomit into the toilet bowl. My stomach has been twisted up ever since the accident. I'm beginning to think this will be its permanent state. Aiden makes me so angry. I keep replaying his words as I stare into the dirty toilet bowl.

It's both of our faults. Is that what he would say to the police? At this point, it would be my word against his. There's no way to prove he was the one driving that night. He could easily lie and say it was me just to save himself.

I dry my mouth and rinse my face in the sink. Even though my vision is blurry from crying, I can still tell I look worn down. I'm exhausted, both physically and mentally. I don't know how much longer I can keep up this façade. At this point, I feel like it would just be better to come out with the truth. I have some money saved up. I can move back in with my family once I'm released. I imagine the relief I would feel getting this over with and clearing my conscience would be worth it.

I grab my phone, which has two missed calls from Henry. I didn't answer them earlier because I knew he would just ask about my conversation with Aiden. Instead, I'll just shoot him a text. I figure texting him now will keep me from backing out later. I need to tell him the truth.

Hey, we need to talk. When can I see you next?

I usually hate receiving a cryptic message like this, but I can't tell him more until we're in person.

I'm free tomorrow afternoon. Is everything okay?

I ignore his question.

> I can come by your place around four. Does that work?

Yeah.

His response is short.

Okay, this is it, Charlie. You're doing the right thing, I try to convince myself. *The truth will set you free.* I lay back in bed and release all the air from my lungs. I long for the day this all ends.

40

CHARLIE

WEDNESDAY, JUNE 27TH: 3:45 P.M.

I'M RUNNING on about three hours of sleep. I've stayed up thinking about what I'm going to say to Henry, tormented by the endless scenarios.

I'd normally be drinking my third cup of coffee right about now, but today calls for some calming chamomile tea. I'm afraid caffeine will only worsen my nervous jitters. I can barely lift my hand without it shaking like someone going through withdrawal.

I've been sitting on this patio swing all afternoon, hoping to calm my nerves, yet I still find myself checking the clock every few minutes. I'm supposed to be at Henry's house in fifteen minutes, but I don't have the will to leave my seat.

Why did I have to send him that dramatic ass text yesterday? Should I come up with some dumb excuse? Maybe I want to talk to him about our relationship. Maybe it's a breakup conversation instead of an admission of guilt.

No, Charlie. You can't back out now. You'll regret it your whole life if you keep lying to everyone. Things will only get worse if I keep up this charade, especially if I wait for the police to show up at my door. At least by turning myself in, I can get ahead of the story and tell them the truth.

I would hate to give Aiden the opportunity to lie. Not that I think he would do that, but honestly, who knows at this point?

I find myself standing outside his door, lifeless. I raised my hand to knock, but it won't move past that, frozen in the air like some kind of salute. Instead, I back away from the door and pull out my phone.

"Hey, I'm here." I shoot him a text hoping to avoid another run-in with Avery.

After a minute or two, the door cracks open, revealing his painfully beautiful face. It makes what I'm about to do so much harder. "Hey, gorgeous." He smiles, looking happier and healthier than ever. "Come in, come in." He places his hand on my lower back and pulls me into his arms for an unexpected yet wonderful kiss.

"Are you okay?" he asks, sensing my hesitation.

"Yeah," I say instinctively. "Well, actually no." My hands must be dripping sweat at this point.

"Let's talk in here." He leads me to his kitchen, where a plate of warm chocolate chip cookies and two mugs of coffee wait for us. "Take a seat," he says as he pulls out a barstool.

I can feel the blood draining from my body as I work up the courage to come clean. "Can I have a glass of water?" I ask, hoping I don't pass out.

"Sure," he says, handing me a glass of water from the tap.

I chug it like a kid who has been playing outside all day, gasping for air when I'm finished. "Thank you. Is this all for me?" I ask, pointing to the treats on the counter.

"Well, you said it was your comfort food, and you sounded stressed in your messages." He shrugs.

Why is he so perfect?

I peer down at the floor in shame, suddenly unable to look Henry in the eyes. This is all too much. I can't hold back any longer and burst into tears. I thought I could get through this conversation, but I'm bawling hysterically before I've even had the chance to say anything.

"What's going on? Are you okay?" He knocks one of his crutches to the floor as he rushes to my side.

"You're just so kind," I manage to say. "You're too good for me." I keep my face buried in my palms.

"It's store-bought dough, Charlie. It's really not that big of a deal."

I try to speak, but the frog in my throat is preventing me.

"Hey," he says softly, "look at me." He gently pulls my hands from my face and wipes away my tears with his thumbs.

"It's not just the cookies." I sniffle. "It's everything about you. You're so amazing. I don't deserve you." I cry harder, sounding like a blabbering idiot.

He pulls me into his chest and wraps his large warm arms around me like a cocoon. I hate myself for crying like this, but the tears continue to flow without my permission. "Shh, shh, you can tell me what's wrong," he whispers in my ear.

I melt into his warm chest, and for a moment, I consider falling asleep here. That would be so much easier than what I'm about to do.

I gently pull away and wipe my tears, trying to catch my breath. "I'm sorry. I have something important to tell you. I just need a second," I huff.

"Whatever it is, it'll be okay," he tries to reassure me.

I close my eyes and take a few calming breaths before trying to speak again. "That's the thing: it won't be okay," I let out. "Neither of us will be okay." My gaze falls back to the floor. There's no way I can look into those honey brown eyes as I break his heart.

"Are you trying to end things?" he asks with a puzzled look on his face.

"Please, just let me get this out," I say. "Don't say anything until I'm done. I really need to say this." My voice trembles, and his eyes grow weary with concern.

"I haven't been honest with you." I rub my hands on my knees, trying to wipe away the sweat. My throat feels like it's going to close soon if I don't speed this up. "I didn't just find you on the road that night."

He leans away from me with a distraught look on his face, as if he suddenly understands what I'm about to say.

"I didn't find you by chance. I was there, in the car." I dry my dripping nose with my wrist.

His face remains unchanged as his brain processes my words.

"I was in the passenger seat when Aiden hit you with his car," I say. "I-I wanted to tell the police the truth, but-but he was so scared of getting caught, I had to make him pull over just so I could get out and help you." My chest keeps seizing as I speak, making my words almost unintelligible. "I'm so sorry, Henry," I choke.

I reach out to touch his arm, but he yanks out of my reach, eyes distant, as if he no longer sees me.

"I wanted to tell you the truth," I continue, "but Aiden hid the car while I was helping you, and then he lied to police. I was scared it would all make things worse if I spoke up. I know it was stupid." I sigh, finally getting my breathing under control.

"I promise, I'm going to do the right thing now and turn myself in," I plead.

His face is pale and expressionless, like he's tuned me out.

"Are...are you okay?" I whisper.

"So you knew?" He breaks his silence. "You were there, and you just didn't say anything?" The pain and betrayal in his eyes feel like a knife to my chest, my heart shattering with a single glare.

"Yes," I say.

"Then why? Why did you keep visiting me?" He knocks over his stool as he jumps to his feet. "Because you felt guilty? Or because you were hoping to get in my good graces in case you got caught?"

The disgust on his face makes me want to tear my skin off.

I stand too. "No, it wasn't like that at all! You were assigned to me by my supervisor. I didn't sneak in to get close to you," I answer honestly. "Then, we started talking and getting to know each other, and I selfishly didn't want it to end." My eyes fall to his leg brace. "I felt guilty the whole time, but for some reason, I couldn't stop myself from getting closer. That's the truth. I didn't plan this to get in your good graces or anything like that." I wipe my face with my sleeves.

"So why tell me this now? Why not just continue lying?" His voice cracks.

"Because," I pause, "I started falling in love with you."

"Oh my God, Charlie!" He winces. "You tell me this now?" He slaps his face with the palm of his hands and mumbles something I can't make out.

"I'm so sorry," I cry. "I didn't mean to hurt you. This all just got so out of hand, and before I knew it, I felt like I was in a hole so deep, there was no chance of getting out. Turning myself in is the only way I can free myself." I sniff, trying to bring back the watery snot running down my face. I dry myself again with the bottom of my shirt.

"No, don't go to the police yet. I just need time to think," he says. "Just leave. I need to be alone," he whimpers. "Charlie," he says as I turn around to leave. "I was falling for you too." His face falls to the floor in defeat.

I somehow manage to hold in the rest of my tears until I get back to my car, where I start wailing into my arms as soon as I'm in my seat. I can't control myself; I'm crying harder than I've ever cried before. I pull some napkins from the center console and start dabbing my face, trying to get the goopy mess out of my eyes and nose.

I feel like he took my heart with him, and I'm nothing but an empty shell.

41

HENRY

WEDNESDAY, JUNE 27TH: 5:00 P.M.

"Was that your girlfriend?" Avery cautiously enters the living room with her laptop in one hand and a cup of coffee in the other. "I heard a commotion but didn't want to interrupt anything serious." She rushes to my side when she sees my face. "What happened?"

I want to tell her the truth, but I don't even know where to start.

"Do you need a glass of water or anything?" she asks, eagerly trying to figure out how to help me.

"N- No," I manage. "That was Charlie."

"And?" she says. "Did she break up with you or something? Is that why you're upset?"

"She just told me something, and frankly, I'm struggling to wrap my head around it."

"Well, spit it out. What did she say that has you so freaked out? You're scaring me." She scoots closer, rubbing my back like she used to when I was a kid. "Don't tell me she's pregnant!" she gasps.

"She was there that night." My throat itches.

"What night?" she asks. "Oh, *that night*. Well, yes, I already know that. She's the one who found you."

"Yes and no," I interject. "She was there, but she wasn't just some innocent bystander like she pretended. She was in the car that hit me."

Avery nods like I said something wrong. "No, no. That can't be right. What do you mean?"

"I mean, she was sitting in the passenger seat when her ex-fiancé was driving, and he's the one who ran me over. She begged him to let her out of the car, and that's when she rushed over to help me. I guess he went and hid the car before cops came." It all sounds fake when I say it out loud.

Avery's eyes darken like she's ready to kill. "We need to tell the investigator. I have his card somewhere." She jumps to her feet and sprints into her room to look for the detective's business card.

"No!" I shout.

She peeks her head out of the doorframe. "What do you mean 'no'? They're looking for the person who did this, and now we know who," she says firmly.

"Charlie said she was going to the cops after talking to me, but I told her not to do anything yet. I want to think things over. This is all happening too fast, and I need time to figure out what I want to do," I say frantically.

Avery looks dissatisfied with my answer and speedwalks back to me. "Henry, this woman has been lying to you from the beginning. There is no way in hell you're letting her off this easy! This entire time, she's been leading you on, all while hiding the truth. How can you possibly be with someone after something like this?" She crouches so she's eye level with me.

"I know, okay? I know it's stupid." I look at her with wet eyes. "Please. Just promise you won't do anything yet. Give me a couple of days to think about it," I plead like I'm a little kid again, begging her not to tell Mom I got in trouble at school.

She squints. "I don't know if I can," she says calmly. "But for you, little brother, I'll try." She plops down next to me and embraces me. "We'll figure this out together. I promise."

I fall weak into her arms, like a child seeking his mother for comfort. "Thank you."

"Now, how about some tea? Why don't you watch some TV? I'll be right back." She tries her best to put on a smile, kissing me on the forehead before walking to the stove.

Charlie's words just keep replaying in my mind. She looked sincere, like she really did regret lying to me, but that doesn't change the fact that she knew what happened and didn't tell the police. She even visited me in the hospital, letting me and all the other nurses paint her as some sort of hero.

And that fucking douchebag who walked in on us the other day... My anger intensifies as I remember his smug little face. I can't believe he had the nerve to look at me like that when he's the one who almost killed me. My sadness is now turning into a bitter rage.

I stand and limp to my room, locking the door behind me. What the hell is wrong with people? To not only hit me, but to insert themselves in my fucking life like this? Pretending to care about me while letting that piece of shit walk free? Fuck this and fuck her! I punch my fist into the drywall. It's such a sudden reaction, I don't immediately feel any pain. I pull my fist out of the wall to see it covered in white dust and spots of blood. I'm going to need to fix that later.

I rinse my hand in cold water and wrap it tightly with some bandages from under the sink. After a few deep breaths, I go back into the living room, where Avery waits with a sad look on her face. There are two cups of tea on the coffee table and an assortment of snacks waiting for me.

"You didn't have to do all this." My mood is still foul, but I don't want to take it out on her. She's the only good person in my life.

"It's my job, kid." She forces a smile.

If I moved to London like she had asked, none of this would have ever happened. Why would I want to live in a desert hellhole like this anyway? London is closer to my old life, and I would be with Avery and the kids. I know that would make me happy. They could spend weekends with Uncle Harry. Their nickname for me since they weren't able to say "Henry" as toddlers.

A warm feeling starts to grow in the pit of my stomach as I imagine being surrounded by my family again. I would love that. "I think I should come to London. I'll start looking for jobs," I say as I bring the cup of steaming tea to my mouth.

She doesn't say anything; she simply pats my back.

42

AVERY

WEDNESDAY, JUNE 27TH: 6:30 P.M.

THAT CONNIVING BITCH! I want to scream at the top of my lungs, but instead, I force a pleasant grin for his sake. My poor baby brother. The image of him injured on that dark road is hard enough, but now, to know one of the people who caused his pain is trying to save her own ass by playing with his heart like this? He's literally been sleeping with the enemy.

I take another sip of tea in the hopes of slowing my breathing, afraid I'll start hyperventilating. I look over at my poor Henry to see his sad eyes staring at the floor, completely lifeless.

She did this, and she's going to pay.

I pull him in for another hug then fake a yawn. "Okay, you look like you could use some time alone," I say. "I'll be in my room getting some work done. Please shout if you need anything, alright?"

"Okay," he says without looking up, expression still blank.

"I'm serious, Henry. Even if it's for something small like to pass you the remote. I love you." I give him another kiss on the forehead and make my way to the guest bedroom.

I barely make it to the bed with how bad I'm shaking. My

whole body is quivering with rage. I plop down on the black comforter and just think.

I know what I should do, but what about Henry? I question myself.

What about him? I snarl back at myself.

He's confused right now. A beautiful woman has stolen his heart and then confessed to covering up a crime—a crime that left my poor baby brother dying in the road!

I go back and forth in my mind, arguing with myself about my next steps. I need to tell the police, even if it means Henry is angry with me. He'll forgive me eventually, he always does.

I pull out my cell phone and search the number for the local police department. I don't remember the name of the detective handling his case and don't know where I left his card, but I'm sure they can point me in the right direction.

"Redwell Police Department," a deep, tired voice answers.

"Hi, I have information regarding the hit-and-run that was in the news. Who could I speak to?" I ask quietly, knowing Henry is on the other side of my bedroom wall.

"One moment please," he says quickly before putting me on hold.

"Hello, this is Detective Sholeman. Who am I speaking to?" an older, raspier voice states.

"Hi. My name is Avery Cooper. I'm the older sister of Henry Ryner, the jogger who was injured in a hit-and-run."

"Okay, Avery. You say you have some information for us?" He sounds rushed.

"Yes. One of the people who was in the car that hit my brother confessed, and I thought you should know. Her name is Charlie, uh, Charlie Damascus I believe is her last name. She's a nurse at the hospital." I know I'm doing the right thing, but I can't help the gross feeling at betraying Henry's trust. "She was also the one who called police when he was hit."

"Would you be able to come down to the station to give a statement?" he asks eagerly.

"Yes. When should I come?" I ask.

"As soon as possible," he says. "Let me give you my cell phone number so the next time you need to call, you get me directly."

"Okay, thanks." I hang up after writing down his information.

"Hey, are you hungry?" I walk out of my room to find an empty couch. Henry must have gone to his room.

Perfect. I'll slip out while he's asleep.

43

CHARLIE

THURSDAY, JUNE 28TH: 12:00 P.M.

I'VE BEEN in bed all day, struggling to sleep. I even called out of work. I figured I'm going to jail anyway, so what's the point? I feel like the life has been sucked out of me.

I roll to my side and stare at the blank wall. Landscapers are outside my window, cutting the grass and trimming the trees, doing everything in their power to keep me awake. Maybe this is my punishment. Just as I start to doze off, my phone starts to ring. Could that be Henry? Does he want to talk?

I check my phone and see an unrecognized number. "Uh, hello?" I hesitate.

"Hi, I'm looking for Charlette Damascus?" An older man asks on the other end.

Woah, my whole name. "Yes, this is she." I quickly sit up.

"This is detective Gary Sholeman with the Redwell Police Department. We were hoping you wouldn't mind coming by the station to answer some questions."

I mute myself to hide my deep, shaky breaths. "Uh, sure, okay. When?"

"Er, preferably as soon as possible," he says, clearly annoyed I even asked.

"Okay. Can I come by tomorrow morning?" I try to mask the pure terror in my voice.

"Yes. Just ask for me when you walk in. Talk soon." He hangs up without saying goodbye.

This is it. This is what you wanted, Charlie. Time to pay the piper. Oh, God. I suddenly realize the gravity of the situation and decide I need a lawyer, so I call the only person I can think of.

"Hi, honey," a soft voice answers the phone. "I'm so glad to hear from you."

"Mommy," I cry out, slapping my hand over my mouth to stop myself from crying hysterically again.

"Honey, what's wrong?" Her voice gets higher with concern.

"I need Uncle Bill," I say.

"Thanks for coming on such short notice." I don't dare look into their disappointed eyes as I open the front door. I can feel my mother and uncle's glares burning into my skin.

"Alright, well, I think we got a good understanding of the situation." My uncle gets straight to business. "The fact that you confessed definitely makes things more complicated, but at least you weren't the one driving," he says slowly, enunciating each word. "Let's get going then. Shall we?" He gestures toward my car in the driveway.

"Yes." I walk like a little girl told to go to her room, face down and feet dragging. My strides are short and slow as I try to delay the inevitable. I'm not ready for this, but I don't have a choice. Justice is coming for me, one way or another.

I feel like I'm on the verge of throwing up again. This whole situation has me sick to my stomach, though part of me is glad to get this over with.

"Remember, look at me before answering anything. I will

nod yes or no, and that will tell you whether or not to respond. Don't surprise me and go off script," he says as he slides into the back seat.

"Okay," I respond.

I buckle my seatbelt in the passenger seat as my mother backs out of the driveway. I think she can sense how nervous I am and didn't want to make me drive. Or perhaps, given the circumstances, she doesn't think she can trust me behind the wheel.

Their small talk slowly fades into the background as I take in the landscape around me. I imagine running away to live in a house somewhere in those mountains in the distance. Just me and my home, unbothered, isolated from the rest of the world.

"Okay." My mom pulls into a parking spot marked 'Visitor' in front of the station. "Are you ready?" she asks, looking deep into my eyes. I can tell she's just as nervous as I am, but she's putting on a brave face, for my sake.

I want to cry again, beg her to take me far away from here, but I resist. "I guess so," I say reluctantly.

We all hop out of the car and follow her inside the station. The place is dingy and cold, several uniformed officers gathered around cubicles.

"Hello," my mother greets an older woman sitting at the front desk. "My daughter is here to speak with Detective Gary Sholeman," she states, as if checking me in for an appointment.

"Okay, please take a seat over there, and someone will come get you in a minute." She points to the lobby then lifts her desk phone to summon him.

We do as we're told and head for the row of black plastic chairs. They're hard and uncomfortable—maybe on purpose.

"It's going to be okay," my mom disrupts my thoughts, eyeing my bouncing knees.

I take a deep breath and slowly exhale. "If you say so."

She holds out her hand, and I grab it. "Thank you for being here. I couldn't do this without you." I smile. I can't imagine going through this alone.

"Charlette Damascus?" A large, tan officer with a bald head walks into the room.

All three of us stand from our seats. "Yes, that's me," I answer.

"Okay, well, we only need to speak with you, so you can follow me this way." He waves me over.

"Excuse me," my uncle interjects, jumping between us. "I'm Ms. Damascus' attorney and will be sitting in on this conversation."

The officer looks at my uncle, whose slender body is too thin for his crisp brown suit, then looks back at me. He huffs, not trying to hide his annoyance, then turns around to lead the way. "Follow me."

The officer ahead of us opens a dark brown wooden door, which leads into a stark white room. Even the floor is white. There's a metal table in the center, with cold looking chairs. I feel like I'm walking through the set of one of my favorite crime shows; it's all so surreal.

"Take a seat, and the detective will be with you in a moment. Can I get you some water or anything?" He looks at me with an expression that's hard to read.

"Yes, water would be good. Thanks," my uncle responds.

The officer turns away and shuts the door without responding. "Nice fella, huh?" My uncle snorts.

I'd laugh if I wasn't waiting to be questioned. I close my eyes and try to center myself. I don't want to let my nerves get the better of me in front of the detective. Just remember what Uncle Bill told you. *Do what he says, and you'll be okay*, I try to reassure myself.

I let out a long sigh. "How long are we going to wait?" I whisper to him.

"Relax." He smiles, trying to calm me. "This is all part of the game. They make us wait to get you nervous, but it's okay. I'm with you, so there's no need to be scared." He gives my hand a gentle squeeze and then moves it back to the pile of notes in front of him.

The door behind us swings open, and I jump in my seat.

"Good morning." An older gentleman with a thick gray mustache walks into the room. He's not wearing a blue uniform like the other officers, instead sporting blue denim jeans, a maroon collared shirt, and a black sleeveless vest. "I'm Detective Gary Sholeman—I believe we talked on the phone yesterday. Thank you for coming in," he says as he clears his throat.

"Now, as I'm sure you know, we got a tip you confessed to being involved with a hit-and-run nearly two months ago. If this is true, I would like to give you the opportunity to share your side of the story."

"Henry called?" I ask.

Uncle Bill loudly clears his throat and gives me the side eye. *Right. Don't go off script.*

"Um, no. It was another member of his family," the detective clarifies.

So Henry didn't turn me in. His sister must have called the cops after I left his house that morning. I don't know why, but that makes me feel a little better.

"So, why don't you get started? Is what I'm telling you true?" the detective asks.

I look to my uncle, who nods, giving me permission to answer honestly. "Yes," I say. "I did have that conversation with Henry."

"Okay," he continues. "Why don't you start with the night of the accident? Tell me what happened."

"Well," I exhale as I drop my hands to my lap to hide my nervous tremors, "my ex-fiancé and I went out for a few drinks at The Hot Spot. Afterwards, I offered to order us a car, but he wanted to drive us home instead. He said the drinks didn't really affect him." I scoff as I recall the absurdity of the statement. "I knew it was a bad idea and should have fought him more on it, but I assumed he wouldn't listen, so I just went with it. He hit Henry on our drive home." I sit back in my seat and hug myself tightly, realizing I've been sitting under an air vent this whole time.

"Um," I say, forgetting where I'm at in my story. "Right. Aiden got out of the car to see what he hit, then came back frightened. I jumped out of the car as soon as I found out it was a person, while Aiden drove the car home to hide it. He ran back after." I look down to avoid the judgment in the detective's eyes.

"I ,uh, called the police to report the accident and ask for an ambulance," I continue. "When they got there, Aiden told them there was an accident but that we didn't see anything."

The detective's eyes shoot up to meet mine. "So he gave a false statement?"

"Well, yes," I answer.

"And you didn't think to correct him?" He raises a brow.

"Um, no. I got scared because he already hid the car. I knew it would make everything look worse," I admit.

My uncle barges into the conversation then. "You can verify what she's saying by checking their phone records. She stayed at the scene to tend to the victim while Aiden drove his car back home before returning to the scene." He slides a couple of documents across the table to the officer. I didn't even realize he was able to pull those up. A perk of being on my mom's family phone plan, I suppose.

The officer quickly glances at the paperwork and continues

with the conversation. "Okay, so why come clean now? Why admit everything to the victim instead of coming to us first?"

I look at my uncle again, and he nods. "Well, I met him— erm, the victim, I mean—in the hospital where I work and got to know him. I felt so terrible about what happened and felt like I had to tell him the truth. I was tired of lying and told him I would turn myself in immediately after I confessed to him."

"So why didn't you? Why did we have to hear it from his sister and not you?" His thick brows furrow.

"Well, she just beat me to it." I smile nervously. I hope he doesn't think I find the situation funny. It's a nervous tick that got me into tons of trouble growing up.

"And what about your ex? You said he was driving the car, right? Does he know you're talking to us about this?" He squints, accentuating the deep crow's feet around his sapphire blue eyes. I can feel him closely examining my body language as I answer his question.

"No, he doesn't," I answer.

"Why didn't you tell him?"

I pull my hair back as I try to think of a response. "Well, I guess because I was afraid he would talk me out of it. He was already upset with me for breaking up with him, and we recently got into another argument about the crash. I didn't want to fight with him about this too. I just wanted to get it over with. I'm tired of the guilt." I lean back in my chair, defeated.

"Is he still living with you?" he asks coldly.

"No, he moved out. His name is on the lease still, but he hasn't been in the house for a while." I play with my fingers in my lap.

"Where is he staying now?" he asks.

"Um, I'm not sure. He never told me." The cold room makes me more aware of my parched mouth. I can feel a sharp bit of dry skin stabbing my upper lip. My finger finds my bottom lip, feeling for the dry patch that needs to be peeled off, and before I know it, I'm tasting blood.

The detective stands and walks out of the room, returning a minute later with a napkin in hand. "Here you go." He hands it to me. "For the lip."

"Oh, thank you. Nervous habit." I dab the thin paper napkin to a bloody spot, and it immediately sticks to my skin.

He moves on. "So, who's car was being driven that night?"

"His," I answer.

"And where is it now?" His head tilts slightly, as if feeling a sliver of sympathy. Maybe it's because I'm confessing with a busted lip and he knows I'm about to go to jail. It's probably an unusual situation for him, having someone admit to guilt rather than lying after each question.

"I'm not sure. My guess would be wherever he's living right now or at his office."

"Okay." He stands. "I think that's all we need. Thank you for coming in. We'll reach out if we need anything else."

That's it? Why isn't he putting me in handcuffs? "Thank you, officer," my uncle says before opening the door to lead me out of the room. I wait to speak until we're outside.

"What's going on? Why didn't he arrest me?" I ask.

"Because, even though you admitted to the crime, they still need proof you're telling the truth. They will talk to Aiden and other witnesses to collect evidence. You'll likely be called back soon to be booked and processed. I know that sounds scary, but don't worry. Your bond shouldn't be high, and I doubt they can get you to serve any real jail time. You'll spend a few hours behind bars at most," he reassures me.

I feel a weight lifting off my shoulders as he speaks. "Well, that's a relief." I exhale.

"They'll likely try to charge you with concealment of a crime and conspiracy after the fact, but I'm sure I can get them to knock off that second charge." He pats my back as we exit the station. My mom follows in silence.

As we leave, we run into Aiden and who I assume is his attorney. We both freeze, staring at one another, unsure of what to say, until my mother breaks the silence.

"Aiden, honey, I'm so sorry you're all going through this. I know things didn't work between you and Charlie, but you'll always be family." She pulls him in for a warm embrace. His tense stature softens slightly as he weakly hugs her back.

"Thank you, Mrs. Damascus. That means a lot." He nods at my uncle and glances past me as he signals to his attorney that they can go in now.

I feel guilty for admitting everything to the cops, but what was I supposed to do? He's the one who got us into this mess. Was I really supposed to jeopardize my entire future for this man? A man who couldn't care less about me when we were together? I owe it to myself to tell the truth.

"Come on, honey. Let's go. We have a lot to go over." My mom wraps her arm around my shoulders and guides me back to the car.

44

AIDEN

THURSDAY, JUNE 28TH: 12:00 P.M.

THIS PLACE HAS a cold look about it. The walls are a dingy white, and the fluorescent lights highlight dirty scrapes in the wall. This whole situation has me on edge, and seeing Charlie with her family outside only makes me feel worse.

I think I'll miss them the most. Charlie and I didn't always get along, but I could always count on her family to treat me like one of their own, since mine was never that good to begin with. We only get together on major holidays and life events.

"Aiden Beckett?" a bald officer calls out, pulling me from my sad thoughts.

"Let's go," my attorney says. "Remember, don't speak unless I give you the okay."

I nod and follow down a hallway into a small interrogation room. I feel sick to my stomach as I sit in the ice cold metal chair.

"The detective will be with you in a moment." The officer with the sunglasses tan line on his face closes the door. An eerie silence fills the room, sending shivers down my spine. They must have come across some damning evidence to have called us in like this. I wonder what it was. Another camera, maybe?

They must have captured a photo of my license plate somewhere. That's the only logical explanation, since there was no one else around to witness the crash.

My palms get clammy as I think over the possible evidence. I think my attorney can sense the tension.

"Just try to calm down," he utters coldly.

It feels like half an hour has gone by, but the clock on the wall says it's only been a couple of minutes. It's as if time slows down in this room, separate from the rest of the world.

The door cracks open, and an older man with salt and pepper hair comes in. His deep wrinkles tell me he means business. I'll bet he's been on the force his entire adult life.

I gulp and drop my hands to my lap, hoping he buys my poker face.

"Good afternoon. Thanks for coming in. I'm Detective Gary Sholeman." The chair screeches against the floor as he drags it from under the table. "I'm assuming you know why I called you in today?" he questions as he sits down across from me. I can almost feel the heat from his legs on my knees.

"Please tell us," my attorney answers for me. I let out a sigh of relief.

The detective shoots an annoyed glance at him. "Well, you see, there was a hit-and-run incident on June 15th at around 2:15 in the morning. Do you recall where you were at that time?" His grayish blue eyes bore into mine, and I almost cave.

I glance at my attorney, and he nods. "Yes. I was on a walk with my fiancée when we found a man lying in the road. We called you guys immediately."

The detective looks down at some paperwork, as if referring to his talking points.

"And where were you walking from?" He raises an eyebrow, as if trying to catch me in a lie. I can feel my cheeks warming under his suspicious glare.

"Um, nowhere specific. We just went for a walk around the neighborhood." My voice cracks.

"Interesting. We have a witness who places you at The Hot Spot Bar with Charlette that night. We already put in a request for their security footage. So, you were either at the bar or at home, going for a walk around the block. Which is it?" His lips tighten, as if trying to hide a victorious smirk.

I nearly choke on my own saliva. I glance at my attorney next to me, hoping he can somehow swoop in and save me. Instead, he just nods again, giving me the okay. What the hell am I paying this guy for?

"Well, yes. We did grab a couple of drinks earlier in the night, but we went home. We didn't decide to go for a walk until later." My armpits are burning up; hopefully, he doesn't notice the dark spots forming under my sleeves.

"And how did you get home from the bar?" the detective continues.

I open my mouth to speak, but my attorney beats me to it. "Detective, we have been cooperative with your questions. Please don't forget that my client came here willingly because he wants to help you with your investigation. You'll also remember he was one of the good samaritans who helped the victim." He stands, his chair scraping against the floor as he scoots it back, just as the officer did earlier.

"Now, if you're not placing my client under arrest, we're going to leave." He gestures at me to follow him. I don't dare to look back at the officer's face, because I know it burns. I can feel his eyes searing into my back as I walk away.

Neither of us speak until we're in the jet black BMW. "This isn't good for your case, Aiden. It sounds like they're gathering the evidence they need to book you and that ex girl of yours. If what he's saying is true and that bar did have a security camera, that will certainly place you there before the accident. Now that they have this lead, I have no doubt they'll be able to match your car to that photo." He grips the steering wheel tight as he thinks things through.

"So what does this mean for me?" My hand shakes violently at I try to buckle my seatbelt.

"Well, if they can prove you were the one behind the wheel that night, you could be facing assault with deadly weapon charges, concealment of a crime, and conspiracy after the fact."

My heart sinks as he lists off the possible charges. Assault and conspiracy? That doesn't sound like me. How can this be happening? I clench my jaw so hard, it feels like it might break.

"Oh, and it's probably best you keep your distance from Charlie. The plaintiff's attorneys could argue you're still conspiring," he says as he revs his engine before thrusting us out of the parking lot.

"Still conspiring? How?" I ask, irritated at the suggestion.

"You two could be planning what to say when you go to trial. The victim's family definitely wouldn't want that," he says casually, unphased. I'm still stuck on the fact that he said 'when you go to trial' and not 'if you go to trial.' Is this really so set in stone?

"Okay, I won't talk to her," I say as I slide down in my seat. I look out the window as he drives me back to Lexi's apartment. This whole case couldn't have come at a worse time. I feel like my entire life is falling apart—first Charlie, then the promotion, now this. I was doing so well. Now, I'm forced to watch as my future derails over a mountain into a big ball of flames.

I know I can't stay with Lexi much longer. She's too nice to ask me to leave, but I can tell she's getting irritated with me constantly being around. I just don't know how I'm going to get an apartment when I'm facing jail time like this.

Maybe I can call my parents and ask to stay in my old room, but that would be like admitting defeat. I'm already an embarrassment for not going through with medical school like my brother, and now, I'm going to be a convicted felon?

"Alright, let me know if they reach out again. Until then, I'll try to find out what they have on you," he says as he pulls up to the curb outside Lexi's apartment complex.

"Okay," I say as I slide out of the passenger side. I stand on the sidewalk, looking up at Lexi's unit, wondering if I should walk in. How will my parents react if I ask to move back in with them? How can I face them after all that's happened? Will they even want to see me after this?

I pull out my phone and stare blankly at my mother's name in my contacts, debating whether I should call. I give in and press the green button before I change my mind.

45

CHARLIE

FRIDAY, JULY 5TH: 12:00 P.M.

I'VE BEEN a sick mess this entire week. I'm just grateful my mother has been here to take care of me. She thinks I have the flu, but I'm convinced it's my body's reaction to all the stress. Any rational person would be sick to their stomach after what I've gone through.

"Tea?" my mother asks as she sets two steaming mugs on the coffee table in front of me.

"Thanks," I reply. "How long do you plan on staying?"

"Until this mess gets sorted. It's not like I have anyone waiting for me at home. Your sisters are out of the house and I'm retired." She laughs. "I have all the time in the world, darling." She gently tucks a strand of loose hair behind my ear.

"Did you tell them why you came?" I ask as I blow at the steam rising from my tea.

"Who? Lilah and Ellie? Oh, no. There's no sense in worrying them. You know how they are." She waves me off, as if I suggested something insane.

"Okay," I chuckle. "I appreciate you staying with me." I lean into her chest, and she welcomes me with a warm hug.

"Of course, Charlette. I'm your momma," she whispers as she pets my head.

Time has been moving at a snail's pace since my conversation with that detective. I've been sitting patiently by the phone all week, waiting for a call from the police. We know it's coming, we just don't know when.

"Your uncle is coming over for lunch." Mom stands and glides to the kitchen.

"Why doesn't he just stay here? He knows I have the room."

"Oh, honey, he's busy with other clients. He would rather have a hotel room so he can still get his work done. He would be too distracted with me talking his ear off all day," she says as she looks through my freshly stocked fridge, courtesy of Mom. She smiles at her work with pride. "Are you hungry?"

"Thanks, but not really. I'm too stressed to eat," I shout across the room.

"Knock, knock." My uncle walks through the front door with a stack of envelopes in his hand. "I hope you don't mind, but I grabbed your mail for you."

I sit up to get a closer look. "Not at all. Thanks."

"Someone showed up today with this, too. Apparently, you've been served." He drops the pile onto the kitchen counter and gives my mother a hug before he hands me a manila envelope.

He sits next to me, giving me a closer view of his balding head. I think the thin, puffy hair on the sides suits him; he looks like some sort of mad scientist. He gently tears open the yellow envelope, mumbling below his breath as he reads its contents silently to himself.

"What are you doing? C'mon, read it out loud!" my mother shouts from the kitchen, where she's cooking something that smells delicious.

Instead, I peer over his shoulder at the summons paperwork.

Concealment of a crime

Conspiracy after the fact

December 3rd.

Arraignment.

Failure to appear will result in further criminal charges."

"So what does that mean?" Sweat begins to form in my palms.

"Well, you're going to go to court, where we will enter a guilty or not guilty plea. You'll get booked and processed at the jail, since they didn't process you at the police station. You'll probably get booked and released," he says matter-of-factly. "I'm sure I can get the charges reduced, since you willingly came forward and brought pertinent information." He pats my back.

My uncle sounds optimistic, but it fails to ease my worries. I wonder what Henry is feeling right now. This can't be easy for him either. I wish I could talk to him again, even if just for a moment, so I can tell him how sorry I am. Not that he would believe me, but still, I feel like there is still so much I want him to know. Where do I start?

I pull out the notes app on my phone and draft a letter.

46

HENRY

FRIDAY, JULY 5TH: 4:55 P.M.

THE PAST COUPLE of weeks have been quiet. Avery flew back to London a week ago, so I'm back to being alone. We got into a huge fight after I found out she went behind my back to the cops, but I can't blame her. I would have done the same thing in her situation.

This time alone has definitely let me reflect on the situation. I even made a pros and cons list about Charlie. I know deep down, she's a good person, and I can't just forget the connection we had. Still, it's hard to move past the fact our relationship was built off a lie.

My phone vibrates in my pocket, and I slide it out to find an essay of a text message from Charlie. My chest flutters when I see her name, and I temporarily forget everything that's happened.

> Henry, I don't know where to start. I'm not even sure I should be texting you right now, given the situation, but I felt like our last conversation was rushed. There was a lot left unsaid, which is why I'm writing this now...

I turn off my screen and stop reading. A lot left unsaid? What did she leave out?

I head into the kitchen and pour myself a glass of bourbon to give me the courage to read the rest of her message. I'm feeling so conflicted right now; I don't even know if I should continue reading or just ignore it and block her all together. A normal person wouldn't give her another chance, right?

I pour the shot down my throat and immediately go for seconds. It doesn't take long until my muscles start to relax. The sweet taste lingers in my mouth as the bourbon warms my insides. The dark gold liquid swirls around my glass like a whirlpool, capturing glimmers of light as it churns. The color reminds me of the gold streaks that appear in Charlie's hair when the sunlight hits it.

I miss her. I shouldn't, but I do. *What's wrong with me?* I look at my phone, debating my next steps. Should I hear her out? My head and heart are at a standstill.

There's no harm in reading her message. I take my glass with me to the living room and get comfortable on the couch before opening the text again.

...I know what I did was wrong. I found myself in a bad situation, and while I tried telling myself I want to do what's right, I didn't. The fact is, I could have fought Aiden harder. I could have told the cops what actually happened, but I didn't. Instead, I followed him like a mindless sheep and took what I thought was the easy way out. I'm sorry for lying to you and breaking your trust. I didn't anticipate you being my patient, but from the moment we started speaking, I couldn't resist the urge to get closer. I felt so drawn to you, and I selfishly wanted to keep getting to know you. Everything about you was addicting to me. I convinced myself it was okay because nothing romantic was happening. I was just checking on the person we hurt.

Henry, I wasn't lying when I said I'm falling in love with you. I truly am sorry for everything I put you and your sister through. I hope someday, we could see each other again.

My eyes stay glued to the screen as I try to process her words.

If I'm being totally honest with myself, I don't regret any of it either. Charlie is a beautiful and amazing woman caught in a bad situation. I'm always talking to my students about forgiveness and empathy, trying to understand others. So what should I do in this situation? Is she genuinely sorry, or would she lie again? I don't have answers to these questions, but I do know I need to see her again.

Maybe talking face to face will bring me the closure I need. Whether or not I can forgive her will depend on what she says.

Coffee?

I write back.

She responds almost immediately.

Yes, that sounds great. The place around the corner from your house?

Sure. When?

I waste no time texting back.

Can you do tonight?

She's eager.

Let's do 5.

I try to keep my replies short. I don't want her to get a read on my emotions right now. *I* don't even have a read on my emotions.

Yeah, that works. Thank you, Henry.

I remember how beautifully my name rolls off her tongue, and my skin breaks out in goosebumps. I miss her lips.

I'm sitting at a round two-seater table by the window. I already ordered both of our coffees. She's not late, but I couldn't help but come early. The lighting is dim with art plastered around the walls. This cafe also serves as an art gallery for local artists, which adds to its charm. They make great pastries, though their stock is pretty low in the evenings.

The bell above the door rings. My eyes shoot up and lock with pitch black eyes—the ones that triggered my infatuation to begin with. I immediately stand, unsure of what to say. All my old feelings come rushing back, and I forget about the sadness and anger I've held for the past two weeks.

"Hi," I manage to say.

"Hi." She smiles and exhales. "Thanks so much for seeing me. I know this is uncomfortable." She sits down, getting straight to the point.

"Is this for me?" she asks as she notices the second coffee.

"Yeah, flat white. Right?" I smile because I know that's her favorite drink.

"Yes." A hint of sadness taints her weak smile.

"So," we say in unison. "Oh, you first." We awkwardly stutter over each other. I close my mouth and wait for her to start.

"How are you feeling?" she asks with sympathetic eyes—the same eyes she had when she first saw me lying in that hospital bed.

"Um, conflicted," I admit. "I feel like I've been fighting myself since we last spoke."

Her eyes fall as her fingers nervously trace the surface of her mug.

"I understand. I was pretty conflicted too. But even with everything going on, I actually feel better. You know that saying 'the truth will set you free?' Well, as cheesy as it sounds, it really has." She smiles longingly, not looking up.

I'm not sure what to say, so I decide to just sit here and wait for her to continue.

"Why did you agree to meet with me tonight?" she asks, looking deep into my eyes as she tries to gauge my reaction.

"I wanted to see you," I say simply. "I know I should be mad, and I am, but that doesn't erase my feelings for you." I lean back in my seat and let out an exhausted sigh. "I guess I just needed to see for myself."

"See what?" she asks.

"I thought if I saw you in person..." I hesitate. "I thought I would somehow know what to do." I plant my face in my palms in frustration.

"And do you?" she asks with soft eyes.

"No," I mumble.

She gently slides her soft hand into mine and brings it down to rest on the table, giving her a clear view of my flustered face. "I don't want to be the cause of more turmoil for you," she says. "You deserve to be happy with someone you can trust with your whole heart. I just wanted to see you again before the ugliness of trial set in." She scoots out her chair to leave.

I squeeze her small hand as if to keep her from running away. "Can you just sit with me a little longer?" I whisper. She returns to her seat without saying a word, relaxing. I want to savor this moment, so we'll just sit here in silence.

47

———

CHARLIE

TUESDAY, DECEMBER 2ND: 8:00 A.M.

Five Months Later

I DOUBLE CHECK myself in the mirror to make sure I look presentable. I guess this is as good as it's going to get. My hair is shorter than before, cut to my shoulders in a dramatic act of desperation, hoping to regain some kind of control. The hospital fired me as soon as they found out, so I've gained a few pounds, since I'm not on my feet as much now. I don't mind the changes to my body, though. It's all part of my new era.

It feels weird returning to the courthouse after so long. I've been trying to shove my fear out of my mind; I don't want to stress myself out, but my uncle is confident I won't serve any jail time. I'm grateful to know I won't be alone in there, and I find a little comfort in that.

"Okay, you ready to go?" He walks through the front door. "Wow, you've really cleared this place out!"

"Yeah! I just finished packing up the last couple of boxes." I smile, looking at my bare house. It's crazy to see it so empty, like a body picked down to the bone. No one would be able to tell Aiden and I used to live here.

"Alright, well, grab your things and let's go. Parking at court-houses is always crazy."

I follow him out, trying my best to keep up.

<hr>

I'm sitting in a long hallway lined with green garland and colorful ornaments, waiting to be called into the courtroom. There's a banner that reads 'Happy Holidays' with a Christmas tree, Manora, and snowflakes. The light-hearted decor does little to cheer me up, though. It's hard to get into the holiday spirit when you're facing criminal charges.

The others who wander this hall look just as worried as me, and I wonder who they are. Why are they here? Are they in trouble, or are they here to support a family member? Or perhaps they're victims of a crime dragged to court like Henry.

We've come a long way since I told him the truth. He was definitely upset at me, but he admitted to missing me while we were apart. That's why he agreed to meet me for coffee that night. We haven't spoken since then, so I'm worried I'll run into him today. I've run the scenario through my head a thousand times, practicing what I would say if we came face to face again.

My uncle is down the hall, flailing his arms as he talks on the phone like a mad man. I thought I would be more unsettled, but I guess I've had so much time to prepare, I'm not as nervous. If anything, I'm slightly excited. I feel like I've been trapped in a room with no doors or windows for so long, and I've finally found an exit sign. It's relieving to know I'll be out of this hell-hole and basking in the sunshine again soon.

My uncle returns to his seat next to me on the bench, still huffing and puffing from his phone call. "Who was that? Another client?" I pry.

"My ex-wife." He groans. "Okay." He slaps his hands on his

knees, changing the subject. "You almost ready? Remember to be honest. Don't try to speak on Aiden's behalf. If you mention him, you can only talk about behaviors you witnessed and how his actions made you feel. Do you understand?"

"Yes." I exhale. "I remember."

"Okay, come on." He leads me into a small room, more like a storage closet, with a single chair and small desk. "A bailiff will bring you in soon. I'll just be outside." He winks as he quietly closes the door, leaving me alone with my thoughts.

I sit back in my seat, close my eyes, and start counting backward from ten. Everything will be okay. This isn't the end of the world, nor is this a life or death situation. I try to calm myself. I thought I wasn't nervous, but now, my hands are beginning to sweat. I really don't want to testify against Aiden, especially in front of all those people, but my uncle says it's the only way I'll get the plea deal. My stomach twists as I picture all those judgmental faces scowling at me as some attorney makes me out to be a conniving bitch.

The door cracks open, and a pair of tired eyes peeks through. "Okay, ma'am. Come in," the bailiff says quietly as he holds the door for me.

I walk past a dozen jurors on my way to a the narrow wooden stand next to the judge.

My feet are numb as I walk. I feel like I'm levitating against my will. Aiden's eyes sear into me as I take my seat, but I pretend not to notice.

48

***

AIDEN

TUESDAY, DECEMBER 2ND: 9:00 A.M.

THIS TRIAL HAS BEEN GOING on for what feels like hours, and all I can think about is how hungry I am. I could have skipped all this commotion if I had just pled guilty like Charlie. On the other hand, my attorney is convinced they have no hard proof I was at fault, which could save me. I've never been a gambling man, but now is the time to put all the chips on the table.

The detective who interviewed me at the station before is currently testifying. "Detective Sholeman," my attorney starts, "you shared evidence with us, the court, that suggests my client's car was involved in a hit and run crash on the night of June 15th. Is that correct?"

The old timer taps the microphone causing a high pitch squeal to echo from the speaker, then leans forward to answer, "yes." His voice sounds strained and tired, like he was dragged out of bed for this.

"Can you please explain to the court how you determined my client was the one driving when the victim was struck?" My attorney asks.

The detective clears his throat into the microphone. "Yes. We had eye witnesses who claim to have seen him in the driver's seat leaving the cantina." He shuts his mouth and sits back, irritated by his interrogation.

"Did any of these witnesses have anything to drink that night? I mean, these are people who were outside of a cantina in the dead of night, after all," he says as he backs away from the stand, gliding in the direction of the jury.

The officer, obviously annoyed, leans forward again. "I suppose they could have had a couple of drinks. We didn't locate these witnesses until much later, so we weren't able to determine whether they had been under the influence of alcohol at the time of the incident," he grunts.

"So, detective—are you saying the only evidence you have putting my client behind the wheel at the time of the accident are a couple of eye witnesses who were most likely drinking and impaired?" he asks aggressively, eyes scanning the room for jurors' reactions.

"We also have phone records that show him fleeing the scene and hiding his car in his garage while the other passenger stayed on scene and treated the victim. She was also the one who called us," the detective points out.

"Phone records," my attorney huffs toward the jury. "Again, that doesn't prove he was the one driving the car when the vehicle struck the victim. It shows, at the very least, that he got into the driver's seat *after* the accident and drove the car back to their house," he says, walking back toward the witness stand.

"In summation, you have evidence showing he was inside the vehicle that night and tampered with evidence, but you're not able to prove without a reasonable doubt that he was the one driving when the crash occurred." He turns around with a proud smile on his face. For the first time during this whole process, I feel a glimmer of hope.

"No further questions, your honor," he says as he returns to his seat beside me.

The bailiff escorts the detective out of the room, and I can't help but feel uneasy as he passes me. He comes back with another witness, and I immediately recognize her cocoa butter aroma as she walks past.

Are you serious? Bile rushes up my throat, and I fight hard to force it back down. Of all the people I prepared myself for, I wasn't expecting to see her face on the stand. Our eyes meet briefly as she settles in her seat, but her gaze quickly falls to her lap in shame. The world around me grows blurry as they do the whole spiel before she testifies.

I feel sick to my stomach by this betrayal. I don't even recognize the woman before me. It's as if she doesn't care about me at all. She's completely wiped her memories of us.

The prosecutor stands to question her.

"Ms. Damascus," a middle-aged tan man in a well-fitted dark suits says, "can you walk us through what you remember from that night?"

Charlie leans forward to speak, careful not to let her eyes wander in my direction.

"Um, yes." Her voice shakes as she responds. "Well, Aiden and I were at a bar that night. When we were ready to leave, I offered to order us a car, but he assured me he was good to drive. I wasn't feeling good on the drive back, and my eyes were closed, so I didn't see the moment he actually hit Henry, but I felt a thump under the car. That's when we stopped and I rushed out to help him."

"So if Aiden was the one driving the car that night, why did you choose to lie to the police?" the prosecutor asks.

"Well, when the officer asked me what happened, Aiden kind of jumped in and answered for me. I know I could have spoken up, but I guess I got scared." Her eyes meet mine for a moment but quickly return to the man in front of her.

"So not only was he driving that night, but it was also his

idea to lie to the police?" He looks around at the jury with scrunched eyebrows, showing a dramatically confused expression. What an ass hat.

Charlie looks around the room, as if unsure how to answer that question. "Uh, yes," she says hesitantly into the microphone.

"Now, while you were treating the victim's wounds, can you tell us where Aiden was? Did he stay with you to help?"

My face starts to burn as he airs out my dirty laundry in this room full of people, showing everyone what a terrible person I am. I take a gulp of water and try to calm my nerves.

"He said he needed to move the car, so he parked it in our garage and ran back to us before the police arrived," she says.

I can see in my peripheral that several jurors' faces have turned sour. I feel so embarrassed sitting here while they shame me like this. I wish I could crawl under this table and just go to sleep.

"No further questions, your honor," he says as he walks back to his seat.

My attorney calmly stands. While I still feel angry and massively betrayed, part of me feels sad seeing Charlie alone and scared up there. I'm sure she's uncomfortable having everyone's eyes on her.

The judge eyes my attorney, waiting for him to start his questioning.

"No questions, your honor," he says.

"Okay, we're going to take a break for deliberation," the judge announces. "We'll call you back when they're ready. Excused."

He didn't have anything else to say? I release a deep breath. *I need a drink.*

49

HENRY

TUESDAY, DECEMBER 2ND: 9:45 A.M.

"Here you go." Avery hands me a cup from the coffee stand down the hall as she takes a seat next to me on the bench.

"Thanks for everything," I say. "I appreciate you flying out here for this." I grab the paper cup from her hand. Her grimace tells me something is wrong. "Are you okay?"

"Well..." She hesitates. "I'm not going to lie, I was waiting to talk to you about something until we were face to face, but now, I'm not so sure. I don't want to add more stress to your plate." She looks at me with concerned eyes.

"Dude, you can tell me anything. What's up?" I gently shove her shoulder.

"Well, this isn't really the place for this, but okay. I'm just worried about you," she blurts out. "I want you to come to London with me. You can stay with us until you find a job and get your own place." The words pour from her mouth forcefully, like water breaking past a dam. She's the type to ramble when she's nervous. "Daniel and I talked it over, and he's totally on board. You can take Emery's room, and she'll bunk with her brother."

"Okay, okay." I hold up a hand. She stops to catch her breath creating the perfect opportunity for me to jump in.

"Listen, I understand why you would be concerned. To be honest, it's been pretty hard for me, being alone through all this. I honestly would love to be around family again, but I would hate to burden you all like that."

I can tell that she feels sorry for me. "Please just promise me you'll keep an open mind. I wouldn't offer if it was going to be a burden on us. Plus, the kids would love to have you across the hall, so it's a win-win." The corner of her mouth lifts ever so slightly.

I look down at my feet as I contemplate an answer. Maybe she's right. There's nothing keeping me here anymore except my job. I can teach elementary school anywhere. I miss my family. I miss having a support system and unconditional love. "Okay," I say. "I'll come." I smile. "After the school year ends."

Her smirk turns into a large grin as she dives in to hug me. "Oh, yay! That makes me so happy, Henry. Okay, let's talk about it over dinner tonight." She lays her head on my shoulder in relief.

"Henry?" a soft voice interrupts the warm moment.

I look up to see Charlie staring at us with wide eyes. She looks different now. Shorter hair, curvier—it suits her. I can feel my sister's grip tighten on my arm as she realizes who she is. I stand quickly to create a wedge between them before responding. There's no telling how Avery will react.

"Charlie... I didn't realize you would be here today," I say, suddenly hyper aware of my movements.

Avery stands, but I wave my hand behind me to let her know I have it handled. She's visibly pissed, but Charlie pays her no mind.

"You look good," she says with a forced smile. "Are you doing okay?" Genuine concern laces her tone.

"A little better every day," I say, trying to keep the conversation short. I can tell by her movements that she's just as uncomfortable as me. We haven't talked since that night in the coffee shop.

"That's good to hear," she says as she rubs her arm, trying to keep warm in this tundra of a building. "Well, I saw you and just thought I should say hi. I really want nothing but the best for you. Bye, Henry," she says. "Bye, Avery," she adds, turning quickly to meet her mother waiting for her at the end of the hall.

50

AIDEN

TUESDAY, DECEMBER 2ND: 10:00 A.M.

MY LEG IS BOUNCING like someone who's had too much caffeine. *Get your shit together*, I remind myself. *This is going to happen regardless, so just sit back and prepare for the worst. You deserve this anyway.*

Waiting for the jury to finish deliberating is nauseating. How long is this going to take? "Sit up straight," my mother whispers loudly from the seat beside me. Her harsh voice echoes through the wide marble hall.

"Right, sorry," I whisper under my breath, though I don't think she heard me.

What if I go to jail? I rub my sweaty palms on my knees, my mind consumed with possibilities. How will I survive prison? I'm definitely going to be a target.

"Try to take some deep breaths," my mother interrupts my thoughts. Part of me wishes I never told her about this hearing, but I needed money for a good lawyer. She's probably already removed me from the family photos on her wall. *'Aiden? That's no son of mine.'* She would laugh.

"Okay." I lean forward onto my knees.

238

The door in front of us swings open, and my attorney walks out with tired eyes. He looks like he hasn't slept in days, much different than the shining personality I saw in the courtroom. "They're ready." He reaches me in several long strides. "Let's go," he says, emotionless. How can he be so cool at a time like this? Doesn't he realize what's at stake here? My life could be ruined!

I clench my fists as I follow him back to our table at the front of the room. My ears and face begin to burn as I feel glares sear into my back. I sit as a line of jurors march single-file into the same seats they were in earlier. The sound of their soft footsteps echo in my mind.

I pled guilty to the concealment charge but not to conspiracy and assault with a deadly weapon. Had I pled guilty to those, we wouldn't be sitting through this right now. My attorney was confident I would be fine, since they couldn't prove I was the one driving that night. I don't talk to God often, but in this moment, I pray the lawyer's right.

"All rise for the Honorable Judge Brown," the bailiff announces.

This is it. What the fuck is going to happen to me? The room grows silent, and my vision begins to blur. I'm feeling over-whelmed and am losing my senses. I see the judge speaking and directing our attention to the jury. A curvy woman in a pink knitted sweater stands to speak. This is it. Listen in. Pay attention, Aiden! Pull your head out of your ass.

I try my best to clear my mind and focus on what she's about to say.

"We, the jury, find the defendant not guilty of Assault with a Deadly Weapon as charged in Count 1 of the complaint and guilty of Conspiracy as charged in Count 2 of the complaint," she reads aloud.

Oh my God. We did it. I'm not completely free, but they

dropped the heavy hitter. Thank God my parents got me a good lawyer. I collapse into my chair, suddenly unable to stand any longer. Muscles I didn't realize were seized suddenly soften, my legs and shoulders sore from unintentionally keeping them flexed the whole day.

51

CHARLIE

FRIDAY, DECEMBER 5TH: 10:00 A.M.

Judgement Day.

I feel like I'm sitting at the bottom of a swimming pool as the judge speaks. Her words are muffled and make no sense. I know I need to pay attention, but I can't seem to get my brain to cooperate. It's like I'm turning the knob on an old radio, trying to find a station that works, but all I get is static.

"Ms. Damascus," the judge's sharp voice cuts through my thoughts. "Are you even listening?"

"Sorry, Your Honor." I jump. "Could you please say that again?"

"You'd think someone in your situation would be a little more interested in what's going on," she says with raised brows. "Charlette Damascus, I hereby sentence you to six months' probation and one hundred hours of community service," she says, looking up at me from her sentencing documents. "Now listen here, young lady," she adds, "you got off pretty easy. I hope this is a lesson for you. Don't just go along with what others tell you to do, *especially* trying to keep a man. Court is adjourned."

My uncle pulls me in for a deep hug, and my mom follows soon after, embracing me from behind. I can feel her sobbing into my shoulder, and it immediately brings tears to my eyes. Is this it? Is it finally over?

I pull away and look up at my uncle's droopy eyes, "What just happened?" I ask in disbelief.

He looks down at me and smiles in relief, like I just won a state championship.

"It's going to be okay. You're not going to jail. You've got a lot of community service ahead of you, though." He pulls me back into his bony chest, where I melt. I wish I could feel relieved, but I don't.

"Thank you," I cry into his stiff polyester shirt.

52

CHARLIE

FRIDAY, DECEMBER 5TH: 10:15 A.M.

For the first time in months, my mind feels blank. No more worrying, no more lying. Just me, alone. I feel like an anvil has been lifted from my chest, and I may float away at any moment.

My mother gently places her hand on my back. "Let's take you home. Your uncle has some business to finish up here." She tucks my hair behind my ears, as if comforting a sick child.

"Thank you," I sigh.

I walk to my front door for what could be the very last time and notice a thin white envelope taped to the center of the door.

"A letter?" my mom asks. "Who from?"

I pull it off the door, careful not to tear the paper, and turn it over to search for a name. It only says Charlie on it, but I immediately recognize the handwriting. "It's from Aiden," I say nonchalantly.

My mother's eyebrows raise before falling, as if recalling a sad memory. "Oh," she says in a somber tone. "I wonder when he dropped it off."

I open the door and walk back into the mostly empty rental house.

"Are you going to open it?" she asks.

"Yes," I say, "but I think I should read it in private." I walk into my bedroom and close the door behind me, sitting on plastic storage container where my bed used to be. I take a deep breath before gently lifting the lip and sliding out a folded sheet of lined notebook paper.

Charlie,

I should have said this to you a lot sooner, but I'm sorry. I'm sorry for everything I've put you through, for blaming you for this mess. None of this was your fault. You wanted to do the right thing from the very beginning, and I should have listened. I guess, like usual, I was scared and chose to do what I thought was best for me. I know you're the one who went to the police and turned me in. I forgive you.

You will always hold a special place in my heart, and I hope we can see each other again, one day. I wish I could tell you that I was happy for you, with your new boyfriend, but I'm not there yet. So, for now, good luck.

-Aiden

I fold the paper and slide it back into the envelope. That's the most vulnerable he's been with me, no dancing around the subject like he normally does. I doubt he would say these things now, though, not after I testified against him. He probably hates my guts and regrets writing those kind words.

A teardrop lands on the envelope, smearing the letters of my name. Why couldn't he have opened up like this sooner? I feel overwhelmed with emotions—sadness for Aiden, fear for what lies ahead, but mostly relief that this whole thing is over and done with.

I'm just happy to finally put this behind us and focus on my new life. It's not going to be easy, being on my own, but I know it'll be worth it.

53

CHARLIE

SATURDAY, APRIL 5TH: 2:00 P.M.

IT'S BEEN four months since the court hearing, and I'm finally regaining some sense of normalcy. I'm living in a small apartment with two roommates who attend the local university. Living with college kids isn't ideal, but the cheap rent is worth it, since I'm relying on my savings for now. The hospital fired me after they discovered the full scope of the situation, saying I broke several hospital policies, though I'm sure it was just to avoid any negative press.

Since I don't have a job, I've been able to pour all my time into completing my community service hours, which is great, because I'll be free to leave this craphole town soon. My mom said I can move back in with her while I sort out my life. Honestly, I'm just looking forward to leaving Arizona. There are too many painful memories here. Plus, I can't risk running into Henry. I'm ready to go back to California and start my life again, surrounded by people who I know care about me.

It's been hard living here since the breakup—not only did I lose Aiden and Henry, but I basically lost all my friends too. Even Sheila's not talking to me. I guess it's understandable, though. Luckily, my roommates, Lucinda and Ashley, have been nice, though they only know about the breakup.

The age gap isn't really a big deal for them; they still invite me out to yoga with them or to get drinks. They're fun and all, but it's challenging to have deeper conversations with them, since they lack any life experience. Their parents still pay their bills, and neither of them have had to work any kind of job.

My phone vibrates on the kitchen counter, and I quickly dry my soapy hands to check it.

"Hey, sweetie. Just wanted to see how you're doing. We miss you!" My mom has been sending me messages like this more frequently. I think she's nervous I'll fall into a depression or something, but the truth is, I'm actually happier than before.

"Thanks, Mom. I'm good. I miss you too!" I quickly type back before sliding my phone in my back pants pocket. I grab my keys and purse off the kitchen counter and head out the door. The girls and I are having a pasta and movie night, so I wanted to pick up some things to cook with.

The air outside is still dry and warm, even though the sun is partly set. I'll miss these beautiful sunsets. They seem more colorful and full of life here, reminding me of an old western film. I think tonight will call for wine and dinner on the balcony; the weather right now is just too good to pass up.

I pull into the nearly full parking lot of the grocery store and pick up a small basket at the entrance. I'm only grabbing a few items, so this should be quick. One of the benefits of living so close to campus is that the restaurants and shops here are nicer. However, they're also packed with students during the school year.

The inside has the vibe of a farmer's market: all the produce is tucked neatly into their own wooden crates, the meat department has an actual butcher, and there are several hot bars lined with an assortment of ready-to-eat meals.

A crate of bright yellow summer squash catches my eye, so I toss a couple in my basket, alongside a shallot and some grape tomatoes. I walk by a smelly cheese fridge on my way to the pasta aisle and stop for a moment to look at the selection. There are so many cheeses I have never heard of before. I'm going to play it safe and stick with good ol' parmesan.

I keep walking, squeezing my way past a blue-haired woman stocking the bottom shelf with glass jars of sun-dried tomatoes. I grab one from the box next to her and keep moving down the aisle. As I look up, I see a familiar figure standing at the end of the row, reading a box of pasta noodles. Shit.

Out of all people, I wasn't expecting to see *him* here. I look down at my coffee-stained tee shirt and sweatpants and suddenly feel embarrassed. Why did I leave the house looking like such a hot mess?

I jump backwards, trying to escape before he can see me, and trip over the employee crouched behind me, falling to my butt in the most dramatic of fashions. Every parcel of food in my basket skips in every direction across the waxed floors. *Ouch.*

"Ow!" the woman yells as she grabs her head. "Ugh, are you okay, ma'am?" she asks once she realizes what happened.

"Uh, yes," I stutter. "I'm fine, thanks."

Henry's face darts toward the commotion and starts walking in our direction, and I only panic more. I frantically roll onto my knees as I try to collect my summer squash before he reaches us, my face down to prevent him from recognizing me. The employee beside me comes to my aid, chasing after a shallot on the loose.

"Here, let me help," Henry's strong yet soft voice says from behind me. I've missed him so much. Shivers rush down my spine, and I hold my breath, unsure of what to do next.

He leans down next to me, grabbing the jar of tomatoes and handing it to me, his large fingers brushing against mine. His eyes look surprised, then relieved. "Charlie," he says in shock as he tries to process the pathetic scene.

"Henry," I huff as I struggle to climb to my feet.

He stands, extending his hands to offer support; I take them and pull myself up. Feeling his touch again makes me weak in the knees, and for a moment, I'm not sure I can stand on my own. He must sense my nervousness and pulls me up the rest of the way so we're standing face to face.

"It's nice to see you." He smiles.

ACKNOWLEDGMENTS

I would like to give a special thanks to everyone who helped make this book possible.

To my loving husband and best friend, thank you for believing in all of my ideas. Your unwavering support, help in keeping me on track with my writing schedule, and willingness to brainstorm with me at the most random moments mean more to me than I can say.

I would also like to thank my sister and critique partner, Misa, for taking the time to read this story through every stage of its journey. Your feedback and constant encouragement are invaluable.

To the other friends and family members who read and helped edit my early manuscript but weren't named. I love you all so much and appreciate you more than you know!

And finally, a big thank you to the Azala team for their hard work and commitment in bringing this story to life.